Peng...
SISTL...

Jean Bedford was born in Cambridge, England in 1946 and came to Australia in 1947. She was brought up in Victoria and after university taught English as a second language and worked as a journalist. She was Literary Editor of the *National Times* and now works as a literary consultant. In 1982 she won the Stanford Writing Fellowship and travelled to the United States to take it up. Jean Bedford's short stories have appeared in *Nation Review,* the *National Times* and *Meanjin,* and a collection of her short stories, *Country Girl Again,* was published in 1979. Her novel, *Love Child* was published in 1986, and in the same year Jean co-authored with Rosemary Creswell *Colouring In, a book of ideologically unsound love stories.*

Jean Bedford lives in Sydney and has three daughters.

Sister Kate

a novel by

Jean Bedford

PENGUIN BOOKS

Penguin Books Australia Ltd,
487 Maroondah Highway, P.O. Box 257
Ringwood, Victoria, 3134, Australia
Penguin Books Ltd,
Harmondsworth, Middlesex, England
Viking Penguin Inc.,
West 23rd Street, New York, N.Y. 10010, U.S.A.
Penguin Books Canada Limited,
2801 John Street, Markham, Ontario, Canada
Penguin Books (N.Z.) Ltd,
182-190 Wairau Road, Auckland 10, New Zealand

First published by Penguin Books Australia, 1982
Reprinted 1983, 1987 (twice), 1988

Copyright © Jean Bedford, 1982

Typeset in Garamond by Dovatype, Melbourne

Made and printed in Australia
by The Book Printer, Maryborough, Victoria, 3465

CIP

Bedford, Jean, 1946- .
Sister Kate.

ISBN 0 14 006496 6.

I. Title.

A823'.3

Published with the assistance of the
Literature Board of the Australia Council.

For Peter, Sophie, Miriam and Ruth.
And to the memory of Ian Turner,
a great teacher of Australian history.

Acknowledgements

This book was written with the assistance of a senior fellowship from the Literature Board of The Australia Council, the only consistent employer of fiction writers in this country.

The main, and invaluable, secondary source for the details of the early life of the Kelly family and the events leading up to Ned Kelly's death, was Frank Clune's classic *The Kelly Hunters* (Angus & Robertson, 1954).

Contents

PART ONE

1

THERE IS A kind of eucalypt that grows all round the district where I grew up, not a blue gum yet its leaves give off a shimmering haze of blue, and it is that blueness that stays in my mind when I remember the day my brother Edward came home from Pentridge.

He was alone. It was late summer; Ned was sweating from the walk from the station at Glenrowan – the first train ride he ever had. The sky was a clear deep blue, the grass lush and green from recent rain; and even my brother's eyes shone blue like the reflection of the sky in a muddy puddle, with a haze about them of distance, and an inhuman quality, too, as if they saw too much and it was an effort to focus in on us, the flesh and blood family, so insignificant we had become.

I was twelve, a young woman I thought myself, and the oldest girl at home since Maggie had married Bill Skillion and gone to live on his selection. We were all there to welcome him: Maggie and Bill; my mother and George King, who was nervous about meeting this eldest son of hers; Dan, myself, Gracie, and Billy; Little Nellie. The youngest ones had run

3

along the track to meet him, to be scooped up by this strange big brother with his growth of beard and staring eyes.

When he came into the clearing I held my breath. Edward had grown tall and husky in prison, and there was that about him now to be wary of. He came straight to my mother and let her weep on his shoulder, looking over her head at us, stretching out his hand for me to take, trying to touch all of us at once – Dan and Gracie, Maggie and Bill – the terrible tautness of his empty, reflecting eyes shuddering for a moment as if he would break down and let the tears gush, then his gaze narrowing as he looked around at us again.

'Where is Jim?' They were the first words that he said, and we had hoped not to tell him straight away.

I looked at my mother. She stood away from him, and her crying became louder still. George King put his arm around her shoulders.

Edward looked at me; I could not lie to him.

'He's taken by the coppers,' I said. 'For cattle-stealing, although it was not his fault, it was because of Tommy Lloyd, and *he* got away with nothing while Jimmy's got three years.' I looked defiantly at my mother. I hated my cousin for going free.

And if ever there was a moment when I could say, there, that's when it happened, that was the point past which there was no going back, it was then, with that fast drawn-in breath of my brother's, the sag of his body before his stare tightened again to its prison blankness, when he muttered, 'Three years. Jesus, three years.' He put us aside gently and walked to the horse paddock. He leant on the fence and gazed at the horses and the bush beyond. It was nearly three years since he had felt a horse beneath him galloping through the countryside, the only sheer pleasure any of us really ever knew.

We stood, a tableau – among the many that recur to me, waking and sleeping – silent, wondering what we could do or say to break the moment. George King held my mother

4

to him; I waited, my hand on Gracie's arm to stop her running to Edward; Dan half turned towards his brother, undecided. It was Maggie who went to him and called the horses over, and leant there with him fondling the soft noses, Maggie muttering to my mother's mare. I caught Bill Skillion's eye in a look that was very like shared jealousy.

Edward turned back to us finally, his face set and hard.

'He will be old and cunning and a criminal,' he said, 'before they let him out again. By Jesus, it's too much for any man, but a boy like that . . .' Jim was fourteen, not much younger than when Ned himself went to Pentridge.

⎔

Two weeks later my mother married George King at Preacher Gould's in Benalla. There were not any priests handy; there never had been when we needed them. Edward gave his consent, grudgingly. He did not like the idea of a stepfather only a few years older than himself, but he believed that Nellie was my mother's child by George, so he would not prevent them marrying. If he had known the baby was our sister Annie's by that bastard Flood, Edward might have committed murder, then. He was anguished enough when he heard of Annie's death – we had said from a fever, and it was, a terrible fever that led her to go with a low crawling creature of the police as my mother said, not able to wait until her husband served his term, with Ned. But she paid for it, in the end, with her blood leaking slowly out of her and no one able to stop it, and the doctor two days' ride away. Annie had the strength only to say she would like the child called for our mother (who was by then weeping, forgiving) before she fell into that deep, waxy doze that she never awoke from.

It was a strange sort of celebration, my mother's wedding, only the family, and we did not tell any others. We were drawing in on ourselves, like a wombat attacked by dogs, burrowing quietly and desperately out of sight.

After the wedding we came back to my mother's house on the Eleven Mile Creek and she brought out some whisky. I suppose the family got drunk. I fell asleep, exhausted, very early.

In the end we did not have to tell Ned anything there was to know about Constable Flood – they hated each other from the start. Flood harried us as he always had, his men always about the property day and night. They came to the gate and inspected everyone who rode up. They stopped Bricky Williamson on his way to and from his selection and searched his saddle-bags. They followed Gracie and me to school and waited at the gate when we came out. It was like a plague of insects – you never could look up and glance out of a window without seeing two or three of the bastards lounging near, their hands on their guns tied over saddles, or squatting, chewing straw, just outside our fence.

Everyone knew that Flood himself and his men stole horses and sold them over the border, and finally the authorities could turn a blind eye no longer and he was transferred. Constable Thom was put in his place, and if ever proof was needed that up till then we had been unfairly persecuted, it will be found in that time. Thom left us alone, and we conducted ourselves respectably. We were finally free to do the work of the property, with Bill Skillion and Bricky helping us, and we began to relax. Edward went timber milling and earned good money. George King helped my mother around the farm, and they had their babies.

Then Edward and George went prospecting, up the George River. Edward always believed our grandfather's boasts that there would be plenty of gold up there behind his run at Glenmore. They took their horses, and the second-hand picks and buckets they had got cheap from a digger coming back from Ballarat, and axes to build themselves a hut.

Again we were a house of women and children, as so many times before, when my father and my brothers were in jail.

Dan was there, but he was hardly home that year, always away in the town with his mates, racing and wrestling and horse-breaking. People still came and went, lodgers again, and travellers staying for just the one night, or my Lloyd aunts and my Quinn uncles – an often bad-tempered chaos of people coming and going, the loud boasting men and the grey talkative women of my mother's family. The yard was always muddy with the prints of other people's horses, the paddock full of too many beasts cooped up together, with much stamping and nipping that had to be constantly attended to. But through all this it was mother who kept it going, the constant core of all the swirling activity. Thin and small, she seemed suddenly old, too, that year. She must have been well into her forties, although she told George King she was younger, and she had borne her share of children and of hardship and of backbreaking work, too.

I was taken from school and put to work around the farm with the horses and my mother's new babies, spending the days wandering down by the river with my little half-brothers and sisters, or breaking and training the wild ponies brought to our paddock by people in the town. It was a time of muddled feelings, at one moment part of the strong rhythms of the seasons and at another, at odds with everything natural and blooming. Dreamy days between the daily work and the child-minding and the horses as I mooned and dawdled about.

&

My brother Dan would sometimes bring his friends to our place, to show off our horses or to rest when they had performed some prank that left them in bad odour in the towns. And that is how we met Joe Byrne and Aaron Sherritt for the first time. At first it was Aaron that caught my eye – the same age as Edward, handsome and hardy, but even then you could sense the weakness in him, the shallow shifting behind his eyes. Poor Aaron – there he forged a link with us that we would live bitterly to regret, although I cannot blame him too much. He was hurt by us many times before he took his revenge – more times than he knew, for he always blamed the Byrnes for Kate's rejection of him when it was really my mother who told them he was in the police pay and they should warn Kate off.

Aaron was a boy who needed someone to admire. Then it was Joe Byrne, gay and charming, that he followed with his eyes. Later it would be my brother Edward, though that may have been because Joe admired Ned so much and Aaron feared to be left out. He was shy with us girls, and romantic, like Joe, thinking that bushrangers were like Robin Hood and wanting to be part of a merry band. At first Joe and Aaron often asked us about Edward, if we had heard from him or knew where he was and what he was doing, although they must have known that he and George King were by now moving stolen horses in the ranges, their gold claim having proved no good. Perhaps it was this knowledge that started Joe and Aaron on their thieving, wanting to prove themselves the equals of their hero, Ned Kelly.

❧

I rode out one day to where Dan and his friends were mending fences. I took them bread and meat and a flask of whisky, and I combed my hair before I started off.

I could hear them before I saw them, and I reined up and led my horse the last few yards through the windbreak to the patch of long dry grass where they were working.

Dan and Joe Byrne were together, their shirts off, sweat gleaming on their pale chests. Aaron, and our cousins Paddy and Tommy Lloyd, lounged around the waterhole, occasionally splashing each other as they lay talking.

I stood still with my horse in the shadow of the last trees, and suddenly Joe looked up and saw me. I had never before thought that a man could be beautiful, and for a moment everything stopped, my horse frozen in mid-stride, my eyes and mouth open, the wind held from the paddocks. He spoke, and the world moved again. But from then on I loved Joe Byrne, and when there is talk of all the help I gave them later and my loyalty to my brothers, no one takes into account that I loved Joe and hoped one day to be with him always.

Joe and Aaron went to prison soon after that, for sheep-stealing, and Dan stayed home more with them gone. I remember from that time the sadness, the awkwardness of a girl too green to approach the man she wants, the dreary dozing days without him, imagining a lover's words, his touch; the dreams that spoil all reality after.

꩜

My brother boasted later that he and George King made a small fortune from horse-thieving, yet we saw little cash from it at the time, except when Edward paid a lawyer once, to get Dan off a charge of stealing a saddle. I don't believe they really made much money from it – certainly we remained as poor as ever, shabby, and, I suppose, dirty too.

꩜

I have never forgotten the look of distaste on the new Superin-tendent, Nicolson's face the day he rode up to inspect my mother's house, having heard so much, he said, about it being a hotbed of outlaws and thieves.

Edward and George were away still, and Dan was off some-where. There was only my mother and me and Gracie and the little ones at home, and we stood about sullenly as Nicolson and his helpers searched the place and carefully examined all the horses.

My mother was particularly outraged because we had had no trouble for over a year – perhaps she had allowed herself to think it was all over. They took an immediate dislike to each other, she and Nicolson. He clearly thought her a slattern

9

and the harbourer of criminals, and what she thought of him she made plain.

'Can't you bastards ever leave us alone?' she said. 'You have one of my sons in your stinking jails for something that was not his fault. Won't you rest until you have hunted us all into the grave?'

He had the eyes of a wolf, I thought, for all his spick and span uniform and upright seat on his horse, and they changed slightly as my mother spoke, becoming for an instant yellow and feral. He was a man who could not bear to have respect held from him.

'You should watch your filthy tongue, woman,' he said. 'You could be put away yourself for using such language to an officer of the law.'

'Law!' My mother spat, and again his eyes shifted. I think he would have retched if the spittle had landed on him.

'There's no law to protect us from the likes of you bullying bastards. If you're planning more trouble for us I hope you will rot in hell.'

'I do not need to make trouble for your sort.' He let his gaze take in our dilapidated house, the sagging fence, our mended clothes. (He had put on his riding gloves to draw back the curtains which divided our sleeping places, and had held a cloth daintily to his nose when he looked behind the beds, while his men sorted through the piles of clothing.)

'You have found nothing wrong here,' my mother said, but she looked afraid.

'Not this time, Mrs Kelly. But I am sure there is plenty to be found, and from now on there will be people watching for it.' He went on, the pompous fool, 'Things in this district have become slack lately, and it is my belief that much of the unsolved crime originates here, in this place.'

His horse wheeled suddenly in a tight circle, and my mother could not restrain herself from jerking forward when she saw how harshly he pulled at the reins. He flinched from her touch as if she was a burning devil from hell, and I believe he truly thought she was. When he spoke again his voice was tight and squeezed out.

'You had best be careful Mrs Kelly. And you had better tell your son and your so-called husband to take care too. They will not get away with their thieving forever.'

He rode off with his toadies in a whirl of dust, and my mother ran to the gate after them, shouting.

'You leave us alone, you stinking pile of dung. You will be sorry if my son ever catches up with you . . .!' But she came back looking tired and defeated and spent the rest of the day in the paddock with her horses, snapping at us if we came too near.

2

IT IS A STRANGE thing that the happy times of my life seem always to have taken place in summer – at the warm turning from spring, the cooling slide towards autumn, or the full burning of the year's end. The summer after Joe and Aaron came back from jail was such a time. My brother Jim remained in prison, growing strange, people said. Edward and George were in the hills most of the time, still without a finger laid on them although Nicolson had hinted they were in danger. It was hot and still, the grass yellow and the gumtrees dormant and shivering in the heat. My mother's babies chuckled and grew and tottered about; the bees rasped and hovered through the glaring afternoons. I was nearly fifteen, my body a ripe lazy seed on the dry land.

Aaron and Joe, always together, came often to stay with us, to see Dan or in the hope of seeing Edward, which they did once or twice when he swaggered in to give my mother money and perhaps stay a night or two. I hoped they came too to see me. Aaron was already courting Kate Byrne, and sometimes she rode over with them for the day and we took food over to Bricky Williamson's, where the boys would help him split rails for his fence for a couple of hours while Kate and I rode along the creek. Then they would join us on the river banks for our modest picnic.

Kate was older than me, and I admired her greatly. She always dressed in strong coloured cottons, making blocks of brightness on the shady brown earth under the peppercorns where we lay and talked and idly watched the men. Kate Byrne watched Aaron, following him everywhere with her eyes, almost in a swoon of pleasure in his company, and I watched Joe.

Joe and I skirted around each other like dogs then, as people do who are young and timid, our conversations jerky and embarrassed, remarks meant to be gently teasing coming out sharp and overloud, shocking us into silence again. I envied Kate Byrne, lying with her eyes closed, her head on Aaron's lap while he stroked her long black hair, his bushman's hat tipped down over his face, only the straw in his mouth moving erratically as he spoke, and his tanned solid hand rhythmically lifting and sliding, lifting and sliding, through the dark curls.

❧

It all ended as usual with the boys, Joe and Dan and his friend Steve Hart, being put in prison again, for assaulting a Chinese who tried to stop them swimming in his dam. But this time I did not sink into misery – there were after all some assurances half given, if only by glances and the occasional brushing of hands. Besides, most of the women I knew lived for long periods without their men; it was not something to worry about overmuch.

❧

In the winter Jim was released. It was as they had said – he had become strange in prison. He was taller, but without Edward's appearance of stocky strength, and he sat silent and bewildered around the house for a few days. Then he left sud-

13

denly for New South Wales, where he said he had friends prospecting.

My mother gave him one of the best of the new-broken horses, and we all went out to watch him ride off in the drizzle along the muddy track. He was like someone who had forgotten how to live in the world, and, sure enough, within the month we heard he had been arrested again. There are some people who find safety between prison walls, after it has crushed whatever there might have been of spirit and adventure in them, and it had broken Jim like a sapling that has to send out its sickliest shoots again to survive.

We heard later that he visited Edward and George up the river and stayed a few days with them, but would not join them when they invited him. He was bent then on his own methods of destruction, and perhaps it was just as well.

&

The winter dragged on. We were hit heavily by the news of Jim's new sentence – three years again – and the rain seemed unceasing. We spent our days huddled into old greatcoats, trying to mend shelters for the horses and the other animals, scrabbling in the sodden hay for eggs, struggling with wet wood and smoking fires. My mother was pregnant again and very tired always. She was too old, and this would be her twelfth childbed, with Johnny still at the breast and little Mary with her weak lungs seeming unlikely to last the winter, which she did not. She was so ill, coughing and feverish, that it seemed nothing but a blessing when she finally gave in and died. My mother had buried too many by then even to weep when the little coffin was taken away on a cart.

The only blessing was that the new hut was finished, and we women and children could move over there, where there was more space and the walls did not leak around our shoulders all the time.

Dan was home again, working outside with Bricky whenever the rain let up, but mostly lounging around the old hut drinking with our uncle Jimmy Quinn, who was out of jail to bother us as my mother said. He was very subdued by now. What had been his youthful sly charm was changed through beatings and harrying in prison to a sort of cowed whingeing. This upset my mother too – she had always had faith in his resilience, his blarney. He was her favourite brother. The loved black sheep. In these months she became truly like an old woman. Her smallness, which had been fiery and darting, now became shrunk in on itself, so that apart from her swollen belly she seemed like a black, bony old crone. It was a time of constant worry for her, and sadness; perhaps she guessed George King was tired of us all and restless to be on the move again.

The rain and cold lasted into the beginning of spring until we were well and truly sick of being cooped up together with the smell of drying baby clothes and unwashed bodies and sweat and bitter woodsmoke.

∽

Then, when my mother was very near her time, Edward and George came home. They seemed to bring with them the sunshine, and everyone cheered up and began to work about the farm again. Dan and I went for our old gallops into the hills, miles away, free at last of jostling bodies and cramped rooms, our horses, too, glad to be out of their muddy corral, working up a sweat through their thick winter coats.

We had been left alone by the police through most of the winter, only the occasional copper like Fitzpatrick riding in on their rounds to make sure we were behaving ourselves, and hoping for a free drink to warm them up.

Fitzpatrick was said to have his eye on me – certainly he came more often than any other – but I had Annie's dreadful example before me and would have nothing to do with him. Besides, I had the thought of Joe always in my sights. They must have been only waiting for the opportunity to get Edward, lulling us into feeling safe.

Edward went into Benalla on a spree; it was a long time since he had seen the old town. Later he said the publican must have put something in his drink because he could never remember being so drunk before on so little grog.

It took four coppers to haul Ned, handcuffed and drugged as he was, before the magistrate, and they tried to have him charged with resisting arrest. Like many of the district judges this one must have had a low opinion of the police himself, for he only fined Ned a small amount and let him go free. But the memory of that scuffle remained with my brother – during the fight Constable Lonigan had grabbed his testicles, an insult Edward found hard to forgive. He always boasted he could beat any man in a fair fight, and Lonigan was a cur, he said, to hit below the belt like that.

After that it seemed best for Edward and George to go back across the border, since the coppers would apparently arrest Ned on any pretext. And so they left again. It was the last time we saw George King, who took himself off quickly when the real trouble started and never saw his second daughter, Alice, leaving my mother with three young babies to fend for. He was surly and restless that last visit, and Edward clouted him once for the way he spoke to my mother.

Joe spent some days with us while Edward was home, and his admiration for my brother was easily seen. He wanted to go back into the hills with them, but Edward said, with a wink, Joe was too young to run with hardened criminals like themselves.

'I'm not,' said Aaron boastfully; he was the same age as Ned. 'Let me come with you. I'm good at horse-stealing, eh, Joe?'

'Not so good that you don't get caught,' said my mother, sourly, and he shut up.

She was happier while Ned and George were there, though

she worried about them. She never cared that they were stealing horses, none of us did. Even the coppers did it if they thought they could get away with it. But now we could all feel the law breathing down our necks with Edward's arrest for drunk and disorderly.

Dan would have liked to go back with them, too, but we needed him too much at home, with Jim gone again. That news had put Edward in a towering bad temper when he heard it, shouting and shaking his fists. 'Will they never let up?' he yelled. 'What do they want to do to us?'

❧

When Edward had gone, Joe and Aaron and Dan became restless and took to the towns once more and their larking about with the Lloyd boys and their other friends. I sulked at their freedom to go off like that, leaving us women and children at home, and I spent long days on my horse practising jumps and rodeo tricks that Steve Hart had taught me. I was hoping to impress them all when they came home again. Poor Steve must have been in prison then – jockey Steve they called him; he was the finest rider any of us had ever seen, and we all prided ourselves on our horsemanship.

We were half expecting it when Joe rode up breathlessly one day to say that Dan and Jacky and Tom Lloyd had been arrested. There had been a wildness about them all for some time, of boredom and inactivity, boys growing into men without much of a future they could see for themselves, outdoing and outdaring each other, eager for any excitement that offered, even with its danger of prison.

My mother sighed and swore and heaved herself painfully into a chair – her baby was due any day – but we did not really worry too much. It was such a foolish charge – damaging some shopkeeper's property and Tom accused of trying to rape the shopkeeper's wife. He was a silly boy, Tommy, and perhaps he made indecent gestures to the woman, but there was little

17

real harm in him. Anyone else but one of the Kelly gang they would have let off with a warning, but our boys they fined heavily and gave three months in prison as well. Even when the shopkeeper was arrested and tried for perjury they did not let our boys out, but made them serve their full time. Anyone else could lie and cheat, but if one of ours put a foot wrong he was slapped into jail and kept there for as long as could be managed.

That summer none of our men were around except for Bricky, who stayed close to our place and did as much of the work as he could as well as trying to fence his own land and dam his creek, and my uncle Jimmy who was no use to anyone. Not that he had ever been, he only sat about drinking and dozing in the shade, not even reliable enough to leave in charge of the babies for an hour or two.

Maggie and Bill came over when they could and brought vegetables and sometimes part of a slaughtered calf and we made some semblance of family dinners in the new hut, the smells of burning fat and simmering beans leaking out into the hot dusty yard where we worked or sat around watching the little ones playing and the old brown hen with her yellow chicks scratching in the dirt.

Joe and Aaron kept away too, and my feeling for Joe shrivelled and waited like the new leaves on the trees in the scalding heat. When he did come he wanted only to talk about Edward. After the fight in Benalla Ned had become even more the hero to the lads, and they all wished he would come back. The Mob was dull without him to look up to and lead them.

❧

One afternoon in early autumn I was inside cooking and I heard Aaron's voice in the yard. I knew he would not be there without Joe so I quickly pulled a comb through my hair and pinned it up behind. When I went outside the men were standing around in a circle, looking down at the dust which

18

Joe was aimlessly stirring with his foot while he told them something in a low, serious voice.

I went over to the men, giving some sugar to the sweating horses tethered near the trough. They looked as if they had been ridden hard and fast, with trickles of sweat running through the dust on their flanks, and the men too were still heaving and panting with exertion while they talked.

'Is your mother about?' Bricky said when he saw me. 'There are warrants out for Ned and George.'

I felt a pain like a cold stone dropping through my chest. Dan was home only a few weeks and already they were after Edward.

'She has gone with Bill Skillion to see some horses,' I said. 'What have they done?'

Joe told us there were men in jail in Beechworth for stealing horses but now the police thought the beasts had come from Ned and George. There was some dirty informer prepared to swear they had changed the brands and sold the horses as straight, so the men in prison were innocent. It was probably true, but that did not make it any easier to bear.

'Jesus. It will kill my mother if they capture Ned again,' Dan said.

He was harsh and bitter those days, with a grudge against everyone after his short imprisonment, always brooding on his injustices, spending his time drinking with Jimmy Quinn and complaining. He did not even go often into town with the Lloyd boys or Joe and Aaron. He was like an animal nursing some internal wound, chewing it over and over in his thoughts, almost, it seemed, coming to love his own unhappiness. He was almost sixteen.

It was decided that Dan would ride into the mountains with Joe and Aaron to warn Ned and George, and although I begged to go with them they would not let me. It was men's business they said; they were excited by the adventure, and they did not want girls hanging about them.

19

When they came back a few days later they said George and Ned were going to sell off their remaining horses (the ones that were not stolen), and go across the border until it all died down. Ned planned to take a coach tour, they said, laughing, or to ride along the Lachlan a bit, see the sights, lay low. Sniggering, they talked of a girl in New South Wales, the first we heard of that, though others spoke of it, later.

George King had given them some money for my mother and a message, saying he would see her when it was safe. If she was disappointed that he had not sent for her she did not show it; by then she knew he would not come back. But we were all relieved that they had been warned and had evaded the police. We did not know yet there was also a warrant out for Dan – he had stayed so close to home since his release we knew he had not got into any trouble. But we learnt soon not to ever underestimate the power of the law to twist and pervert the truth to serve its ends, nor to be surprised at the depths of greed and degradation of the police themselves – something we thought we already knew about.

❧

Constable Fitzpatrick was one of the scum of the earth. How people could say there was anything between us I do not know. Even his fellow coppers found him loathsome. He was a drunk and a liar and a braggart, and I believe he was deliberately left in charge of the station at Greta while the warrants were out for my brothers. Wolf-eyed Nicolson was hoping to kill two birds with one stone. Knowing Fitzpatrick was indiscreet and stupid, Nicolson hoped there would be some furore which he could turn to advantage, and he would be satisfied before they were done.

Fitzpatrick rode up one afternoon just as we finished our midday meal. I was in the yard throwing dirty water behind the shed, the babies tumbling about with the dogs beside me.

I thought little of seeing him there for the police had been nearly every day since the warrants were out for George and Ned, searching the huts, inspecting the horses for old brands, generally hounding and upsetting us as they knew well how to do. Fitzpatrick thought he was enough of a regular at my mother's to be safe coming by himself – usually they came in twos and threes, frightened I suppose that our mother or us girls would attack them. We thought then nothing could increase our hatred and contempt for those men, but we were wrong.

My mother came out when she heard the horse. She thought it was Dan back from looking at stock in Winton. She stood, her raised arm shielding her face from the sunlight, watching as Fitzpatrick dismounted. You could tell he had already had a few grogs by his unsteady swagger.

'Where is Dan?' he said to my mother, peering under the verandah to try to see her face.

'Why are you here?' My mother's voice could be cold and lashing. 'Can't you find honest work? Do you have to earn your pay frightening children and old women?'

'Now, now, missus.' He was a whining drunk, like many Irishmen, my own family included. 'Don't take on. Where is your son? I need to have a word with him.'

'He is off doing decent work, not like you. Why don't you get an honest job yourself? You are a young man, it is probably not too late. But then,' she stared at him, 'maybe it is, for the likes of you.'

He became angry. 'I wish to speak with Dan Kelly.'

Bricky came out of the men's hut, wiping his hands on his shirt. My uncle, behind him, darted back when he saw the policeman.

'What do you want with Dan? He's done nothing wrong has he?' Bricky was a shy man but he could speak up to defend his friends.

'That's between me and Dan Kelly.'

21

Fitzpatrick turned and got back on his horse. 'I will be back later, tell him.'

My mother jerked her head in contempt at the ridiculous man fumbling with his reins. We still did not realise that he could mean serious trouble for us.

Bricky went off to split timber on his own land and we forgot about Fitzpatrick. Dan and Bill came home in the evening with the horse-dealer, Burns, and a neighbour, Joe Ryan, and my mother told them the copper had been there. My brother's sulky face became red with anger.

'Why won't they leave me alone?' he said. 'What have I done now?'

'They are hoping you will tell them where Ned is,' said Bill sensibly. 'Don't get too worked up about it.'

My brother turned abruptly and went into our hut to wait for his dinner. Bill and Joe Ryan left and said they would come back later.

Just as they rode away we saw Burns coming from the old stockyard with Fitzpatrick again on his horse.

'Jesus Christ,' Bricky said. 'What does the bastard want now?'

Dan came out again and stood with his arms folded, waiting for them to come to the steps. Fitzpatrick was too drunk to dismount properly, and I had to hold his horse still for him.

'Well?' said Dan aggressively. 'Why are you hounding me?'

'You are wanted in Chiltern for horse stealing.' Fitzpatrick blurted it out and we all stared at him in disbelief. He seemed frightened then at what he had said, but he repeated it.

'Someone has given evidence that you and Jack Quinn were seen driving horses that were not yours,' he said, swaying back towards his horse in apprehension, or drunkenness. I think myself he was too far gone in drink to realise what he was doing.

'You are bloody mad, you bastard,' Dan shouted. 'I haven't been near Chiltern for months as you well know. You're trying to trick me into your rotten prison again, but this time I will not go.'

The fool became ingratiating. 'Now, now. I think we can come to some arrangement. At least you must come to town to answer the charges. We can soon prove them wrong.'

He moved towards Dan, smiling his false smile, but Dan brushed him off roughly. Bricky took my brother's arm.

'Dan, they can't prove anything. There are many of us to swear you haven't been in Chiltern. Keep calm and you will spoil their game.'

My brother looked confused, but he trusted Bricky's judgement.

'All right,' he said sullenly. 'I'll come with you only to answer the charge. But you'll have to wait until I've eaten my dinner.'

The policeman was delighted. 'Sure, that's fine,' he kept saying. 'That's fine. I'll just come in and warm myself by the fire while I'm waiting, shall I?'

'If you must. We cannot stop you,' my mother said, but he was not capable of noticing her hostility. It was growing dark and we were hungry. I suppose the men thought if they could get him any drunker they might persuade him to leave without Dan. We went inside.

While we ate he sat by the fire drinking and trying to stay on friendly terms with us. He did not understand that we watched him as kookaburras might watch a snake, hoping to strike before the venom is released, then battering it to death with their heavy beaks.

Later in the night Bill Skillion and Joe Ryan came back and sat quietly watching and drinking, filling up Fitzpatrick's mug whenever it was empty, listening to his bragging about the cunning of the police and how they would take all the horse thieves before long.

'We have a plan,' he was slurring his speech, his eye winking confidentially. 'Superintendent Nicolson – there's a wily bugger for you. There will not be a horse thief left in Victoria if he has his way.'

But he was not privy to any real plans – Nicolson was too clever to trust the likes of him with anything but the dirty jobs that suited him. We let him talk.

Finally he got up and told Dan to come with him. My mother could not contain herself any longer and demanded to see the warrant.

'It's back at the station,' he said.

'Then Dan will not go with you. When you bring the warrant then we'll see.' Her voice trembled with anger.

'You'll see something all right,' and he dived into his pocket and brought out his revolver, waving it in the air so that we were all in danger of being shot, even the babies on the floor. My mother's rage could no longer be suppressed. She picked up the heavy fire shovel from the grate and raised it over her head.

'You put that gun away or I will dash out the little brain you have,' she shouted. 'If Ned was here he would ram that bloody thing down your miserable throat.'

He faltered, and I think my mother was disappointed. In that moment she would have thought hanging well won if she could beat that man to death. Bricky and Bill took the gun away from him and sat him down again, not gently. My mother put back the shovel with shaking hands, but stayed close to it.

'Forget it, man,' Bricky said. 'We are all a bit the worse for drink. Let it go.' He gave him another mug of whisky and we relaxed when he took it and began to drink again.

'All right,' he said, 'All right. I'll go now, but I will come back tomorrow with the warrant.' He winked at Dan.

'If you want my advice, boy, you will join your brother in the bush. Run off and let them sort it out without you. If you are innocent you will soon be able to come back.'

It was stupid advice from a stupid man, as we tried to tell Dan after Fitzpatrick had finally staggered off, but my brother was young and terrified of going to prison again, and he would not listen to us. It is a terrible irony that when that case did come eventually to court Jack Quinn was completely acquitted, and so would my brother have been. But by then it was too late.

We should have killed Fitzpatrick. The next day he came back with other troopers, and they took away the lot of them. Like the cowards they were they waited for dark, taking Bricky as he went back to his hut after dinner, quietly, so that we didn't hear. Then they went over to the Skillions' and woke Bill out of sleep, with Maggie and the frightened children watching as they led him off. For my mother, the terrible Mrs Kelly, they surrounded the house and moved in like an army at dawn, waking us all, driving her off in the cold morning, the baby at her breast and the little ones crying and calling after her. My brother Dan had gone in the night; our uncle Jimmy Quinn had disappeared. Gracie and I were left alone, two anxious grieving girls and the babies.

Fitzpatrick swore that we had tried to murder him, although they never, then or later, found the revolvers Bill and Bricky were supposed to have threatened him with, nor any trace of Ned who Fitzpatrick claimed had tried to shoot him – which was not surprising since Ned was hundreds of miles away in New South Wales.

Everyone knew Fitzpatrick was a liar and a scoundrel but it suited them to pretend to believe him, even despising him as they did. They were bent on destroying us – like a nest of rats the farmer comes on with his plough – not caring that they hurt women and children but only wanting to root us out completely.

3

THE DAY AFTER my mother was taken away Maggie moved in with us again, pale and grim with the shock of Bill being forced from her like that.

'A man who never harmed a fly,' she said, the tears dripping down her face.

And, as Ned said later, Bill and Bricky hardly knew a gun from a pot handle. And where would they have got revolvers from anyway as the liar Fitzpatrick said they had? And if they had them, what did they do with them after?

Not all the coppers' searching could ever find a trace of weapons, yet Constable Flood testified at my mother's trial that he made moulds from bullet holes found in our house. I don't even recall seeing him near the place during that time, although knowing him, he might have sneaked in some time when we were not there. It makes my heart beat fast and my hands tremble even now when I remember how we were treated then, girls and babies, how they pushed us around and shouted at us, shoving us like dogs out of their way when they came with their guns to search our place.

I still do not know what they hoped to find. Perhaps some

of them believed Fitzpatrick's tale of revolvers and attempted murder, though they said they were searching for clues to Dan's whereabouts and proof that Edward had been there. Whatever it was, they did not find it in the drums of overturned and broken eggs, or the spilt flour, or the pickled meat slopped out and left seeping into the mud of the floor. Maggie followed them about as they destroyed our food, trying not to cry, forcing herself to beg them to leave us enough to live. They took no notice. To them we were vermin, and our destruction was inevitable.

'It's little Kate,' Fitzpatrick would say when they dismounted, ten or twelve of them sometimes, cocky and strutting when they had their guns and each other to give them heart.
'Come here then, and hold my horse for me. She's the best of the bunch, aren't you girl?' They all laughed when I tried to spit with my mother's fierceness.

'A wild little colleen she is, to be sure.' How I hated his whining voice.

I never told Ned how Fitzpatrick would try to take my arm, or try to make me kiss him while I writhed and struggled. Ned was enraged enough when he heard how they spoilt our provisions and pushed us roughly about. I think he would have rushed off immediately to kill Fitzpatrick if he thought he'd lain a finger on one of us. I will say it for some of the police though, that while the other low rats laughed and egged him on, there were one or two that told him sharply to try and behave like a man, hard though it might be for him.

When he let go of me I would run sobbing, nearly choking, into the scrub, clambering up the overgrown hillocks, burying myself deep inside the prickling undergrowth where I could cry and shudder to my heart's content. Once I crept back too soon and they were still there, with the family mustered in the yard, though my uncle Jimmy, as usual, was nowhere to be seen. Strahan and puffed-up Smith and Fitzpatrick had their guns pointed at my sisters who stood frightened and defiant, not moving.

'We should shoot the lot of you.' It was Fitzpatrick. He was drunk; I had smelt the whisky on his foul breath when he grabbed me by the waist and tried to hold me.

'Tell your famous brother that we will shoot him like a dog if we ever find him. We will blow him into pieces.'

Maggie had some of my mother's steel although she was terrified – any of those fools might have accidentally discharged his gun and killed one of the children.

'When my brother Edward finds out the way you have treated us, there's not one of you will lie safe in his bed.' She glared at them. 'That is a promise. If he was here you'd run for your lives, you cowardly scum.'

Strahan made a threatening move towards her, but other troopers came from behind the house and put a stop to it. After they had ridden off, cooeeing and whooping like children, I went inside and found Maggie sitting at the table, white and shaking. She was small and indestructible, like our mother, but that time she came near to breaking.

'What shall we do, Kitty?' Her hands twisted repeatedly at the long hair that had come out of its bun, falling in wisps around her shoulders. 'We must get word to Ned somehow, but he must not ride into a trap.'

She was bearing the whole load of our family – our uncle Jimmy Quinn was no use to us, more of a burden, hardly able to look after himself any more, and we were afraid to contact Dan too openly in case the coppers followed us to his hideout.

I said I would ride up to where Dan and Wild Wright were camped in the hills and see if they had word of Ned. I was sure I could outride any policeman who tried to follow. Maggie did not like it but we had no choice. The word had not yet got round. Later, many would come to our assistance and we would never want for messengers and spies on the police camps, but we did not know then it would come to that.

☙

Dan and Isiaih Wright were camped at Bullock Creek on one of the old claims that Ned and George King had once tried to work – Isiaih was sure he could get gold from the river. On the way there I called in at Glenmore to tell our Quinn relations what we were doing. They said they would try to raise some money for my mother's bail – her hearing was in another week or so. They'd become respectable, by our standards, the Quinns of Glenmore, now that Jimmy was gone and the Lloyd in-laws had moved out to their own runs. But the old hatred of the law was still there and they rallied angrily to protect their own. My uncle Pat Quinn offered to ride with me but at that stage we did not want anyone else to know the exact place of the hideout. He said he would go over to our place at Greta to see if Maggie needed help.

Despite the anxiety always at the back of my mind, riding in those hills on Oliver Twist always gave me pleasure. Cantering into the ranges that early morning, the mist lifting in sheets from the grass, the horse's breath frosting in the air, I splashed back and forth across the creek – to muddy the trail, I said to myself, but really for the sheer pleasure of it, lying low on the horse's back, galloping full stretch along the cleared banks, wheeling and twisting through the denser bush near the camp.

Dan and Isiaih had fixed an old rough hut of slabs and mud and cleared some ground. They seemed very settled, Dan proudly showing me the growing feed for the horses and the specks of gold carefully washed and wrapped in soft chamois.

Dan seemed happier than he had for years. He was born to be a farmer – working with animals and with the land were his two great skills. Wild Wright, Isiaih, was, as usual, large and blustering, amusement always lurking in his eyes. I told them about my mother's arrest and watched the contentment drop from my brother's face like a slipping mask.

'Does it mean I'll have to go back?' I do not know what had happened to him in his short time in prison, but he had a mortal fear of returning.

Isiaih shook his head.

'No. We'd best get word to Ned and see what he thinks. It'll do no one any good to have you behind bars as well.'

My brother's relief made me worried. He would do anything rather than be put away again.

I unpacked the flour and dried meat they gave me at Glenmore and we made damper and sat around the fire eating and talking until it was dark and the stars glinted in the deep clear sky. I lay in the open between the men, beside the banked smouldering coals, my mind too cold and exhilarated to allow me to sleep until it was nearly dawn.

My mother was the only one to get bail – perhaps they relented at the thought of the baby spending that winter in prison – and we managed to raise the money among our relations and friends.

She came home for a few months. The trial was set for spring, and Maggie and I tried to comfort her and feed her up to withstand the prison term we still hoped she would not serve. She had become very silent, although her black eyes still flickered fiercely, especially if anyone spoke of the trial or of her sons.

With her at home the coppers intensified their watches. I suppose they hoped Ned would come riding in to see his mother, which he did, but they never knew about it. Once he came dressed in my aunt Kate Lloyd's clothes, and they never even saw him, let alone recognised him. Or he would come in the dead of night, leaving his horse tethered far up the river, coming down silently through the trees and around the coppers' camps where they snored and grunted. We would wake to find him asleep on a blanket in the kitchen. He was jumping with frustration those days, not knowing whether to give himself up to prove his alibi for the Fitzpatrick case or to stay in hiding in case they tricked him again. He had to settle for pressing money on my mother for the lawyers, sending money to the jail for Bricky and Bill and taunting the police with sudden appearances in the townships, which they never could verify, him being miles away before they even heard of it.

In the spring they took my mother away again to await trial. She went silently in the police cart, sitting up straight, the baby in her lap.

'I'll show them that us Kellys can behave with pride, she said, 'even if they cannot.'

Ned was camped now with Dan and Wild Wright, and although Maggie and I often rode out to see them and sometimes caught sight of coppers on the way, none ever seriously tried to follow us. I think they had a fair idea all along where my brothers were, but were too craven to try and capture them without an army.

Edward had been talking with the lawyers about my mother's case and had been persuaded it was hopeless unless he could prove his own alibi. The evidence rested on whether he had been there or not, and if so whether he had shot at Fitzpatrick.

Finally Isiah and my uncle Pat Quinn rode down to Beechworth saying that Ned and Dan would give themselves up on their previous charges and face the present one if my mother could go free. I do not know what Ned did to make Dan agree to this, but it was probably the bravest thing he ever did, given the way he felt about being shut up again in their prisons.

The magistrate that spoke to Isiaih and Pat seemed sympathetic, Isiaih said, and impressed by my brothers' offer, but he could not promise anything, and my brothers could not see the point in allowing themselves to be captured if it would not ensure our mother's release.

There was great business at that time in the police force about the general lawlessness and the incompetence of the coppers, and that was why tyrants like Nicolson were prowling about trying to arrest everyone they could lay their hands on, to prove the police force was effective. It was in their interests to make out my brothers were violent and dangerous outlaws. Their wages would go on being paid if they could prove to the people that they needed protection from such wild beasts as our family.

We all rode down to Beechworth for my mother's trial, except for my aunt Kate Lloyd who brought the children in the train, a great excitement for the little ones who had never been on it before.

For four days we sat in the courtroom listening to the lying bastard Fitzpatrick swear that my brother Ned had tried to shoot him and that my mother had nearly killed him with the shovel. I watched their faces, the magistrates and the policemen and the sober men of property, and I did not understand how they could bring themselves to believe this drunken braggart who lolled in the witness box and leered and winked and had to be prompted many times before he got his story straight.

By contrast, my mother and Bill and even poor scared Bricky sat quiet and proud, neatly dressed and clean and did not falter in their stories, which were pretty well the truth, although perhaps they exaggerated their innocence a little, not mentioning the real violence that lay in all our thoughts that night.

Some farmers gave evidence to the men's character and attempted to give Bill an alibi for that night, but they were not listened to. The publican at Winton said Fitzpatrick was sober and wounded when he saw him riding back from our place that night, a lie that had even the other coppers smiling sourly at each other, who knew he never had a sober day in his life. But that lie was believed.

The monster Judge Barry, like a poisonous toad all bloated up with his own importance since he became a Sir, sat in his high chair like an overfed and spoilt infant, fidgeting and belching and peering maliciously at my mother whenever her name was mentioned. He hated us, it was clear, and he could not wait for the verdict of guilty to be brought in before he began his threats.

He pronounced the sentence with pleasure, it seemed, taking time to deliver homilies and self-congratulation, and finally saying that he thought it would be good for everyone to have some of the notorious Greta Mob behind bars. (Three people who were part of no Mob at all, then or later.) Then he said he was sorry he did not have my brother Edward Kelly there, for he would like to give him fifteen years and make an example of him once and for all. It was cruel and unnecessary at the time, but no one came forward to tell us that in law he should not have been allowed to say such a thing about a man not yet arrested, let alone found guilty, and should certainly not have been allowed to preside at my brother's trial later, having said it.

My mother, with her infant, was sentenced to three years in Pentridge, and Bricky and Bill six years apiece.

'Oh God, Oh God, what shall we do now?' Maggie wept then, but she was calm when she was allowed to see my mother before they took her away. My mother was stricken and shrivelled, but she managed to give instructions about the property and pass on messages from Bill about the running of the Skillions' place while he was away. She had been told about Ned's offer to the magistrate and said it was just as well he was not taken up on it.

'From what they have done to us here, today, it is certain your brothers would never see daylight again if they were caught. Tell them to get away, overseas if they can. They can do no good hanging about here.'

It was good advice, but my brothers were honourable in their own way, and they would not rest until they had taken revenge for our mother's treatment. I was the one who took her message to the camp under the gumtrees, and I saw Ned's terrible face.

'That's that, then,' he said. 'We will give them a run for their money now, all right. They will learn they cannot treat us like dogs forever, but that even the meanest cur will turn and bite if it is pushed too far.'

I agreed. I was glad they would not run away and leave things as they were. I was young and silly, but what had happened to my mother seared very deep.

'Let me come with you,' I said. 'I want to live here with you and help you fight them.'

Edward did not laugh, but he said, 'No. You're needed at home, Kitty. Maggie can't do everything herself.' He put his arm heavy on my shoulders. 'But you can come and stay with us sometimes. You will help us more, too, by reporting to us about the coppers.'

☙

The very next day the police came in greater strength than ever before to our place and told us there would soon be an armed force out hunting our brothers. They swaggered and boasted about our yard, squabbling about who would be the first to shoot Ned Kelly, how they would riddle his body with bullets so that not even his family would recognise him after.

Finally they rode out, but Fitzpatrick fell behind and backed his horse over to where I stood in the paddock. I tried to slip under the rails, thinking he was up to his usual tricks, but his voice stopped me. For once he seemed sober, and his pasty face was serious.

'I'm going away soon,' he said. He looked embarrassed, even ashamed.

'I'll miss you Kate. D'you know what I mean? There are no hard feelings I hope? It was all in the line of duty you know.' That wheedling Irish voice.

'You're wise to leave,' I said. 'My brother would kill you if you stayed, for what you've done to us.' He looked over his shoulder furtively as if he expected to see Ned ride up then and there.

'He might come after you anyway,' I said, seeing his fear. 'Wherever you are he might find you and slit your lying throat. And I hope I am there to help him.'

I bent quickly around the horses and ran out of the paddock into the bush. From my hiding place I watched him wheel his horse then hold it still for a moment, trying to see where I had gone before he galloped off after his cohorts, calling to them anxiously to wait.

4

MAGGIE WANTED TO be the one to warn our brothers of this new danger, but I knew Joe was at the camp with them and I nagged until she gave in. She guessed why I was so anxious and tried to warn me.

'It's foolish,' she said. 'He is not ready to settle, he'll be a larrikin for a while yet. You should wait a year or so before you thrust yourself into his notice.'

I pretended I did not know what she meant and wept and stormed until she agreed. She was only twenty-two then but the lines were already deep in her forehead and beside her full mouth. People who knew her later said she must have been a great beauty, but she was not. Her life was too hard and she came to know grief too young.

'Take care,' she said when I rode off, and I knew she meant more than to watch out for the police.

'I will,' I said. I could not stop smiling. She knew more than I did, certainly, but if I had not grabbed my chance at happiness then it would have been too late. Neither of us could have known that.

I rode and rode. I did not stop at the Quinns', although it was not far off the track. I told myself it was the urgency – the police troop was already mustering at Mansfield. It was urgent, but I didn't give a damn for the police. When my horse sweated and began to gasp I slowed down to an agonising walk. I stood beside him when he drank, impatience burning in me like a fever, feigning calm so that he would be calm, too, and ready to gallop again. He was winded when I arrived at the camp, nearly ruined, his thick lips drawn back in a sneer of exhaustion.

Dan ran out of the hut and looked at my horse.

'Jesus,' he said. 'What has happened?'

I laughed, and he looked at me with hostility. We were never easy together, too close in age, too quarrelsome.

'Where is Ned?' I said. I meant, where is Joe Byrne.

'They're up the river a bit. We've built a still.' He smiled, a sly smile like our uncle Jimmy's. I laughed again.

'You needn't laugh,' he said, sullen once more. 'Look.'

We walked to the clearing beside the hut. The feed was two or three feet high, sturdy and leafy.

'So?' I said. 'Lucerne. You'll not make whisky from that.'

'It's not lucerne,' he said, very pleased with himself. 'It's mangel-wurzel.'

Now we both laughed.

'Joe and Aaron will sell it for us,' he said, his soft face full of cunning and pleasure. 'We'll make a fortune, much more than with the gold.'

'Our mother never made her fortune,' I said, and he stopped smiling.

'She didn't know how to sell it properly,' he said, 'with the most profit to herself. She even gave it away if she was sorry for the man.'

He bent and pretended to firm the earth around the plants. His voice was reluctant and slow.

'Well? How is she? Is there bad news?'

37

'No, not of our mam,' I said. 'It is worse than that. You'd better take me to where Edward is.'

◦

They had built the still in the undergrowth nearly half a mile from the camp. When we found them they were just pulling back the branches over it – you could not see it at all when they had finished. Ned, Steve Hart and Joe. They stood for a moment looking at their work, making sure they had hidden it well before they turned to me.

I could not tear my eyes from Joe's – we both knew somehow it was time. I had chosen Joe Byrne long before that day but this was the first time he acknowledged it. Now I am filled with guilt. I delivered the message to my brother, yes, but my heart was not in it. Perhaps – it is one of my many perhaps's – perhaps if I had not been so besotted with Joe, if I had made my message clearer, it would all have been different. I don't know. I don't know, and it destroys me still.

When I told them what the coppers had said, and that they were massing a hunting party from Mansfield, Edward said simply, 'Yes, we know that already'. Wild Wright had been up to the camp and had ridden back in haste to see what else he could find out.

'But they mean it this time,' I said. I did try – but was it really the warning that concerned me or did I only want to impress Joe? 'They say you are to be taken, alive or . . . dead.'

We walked back to the hut, I with my arm in my big brother's, my whole body leaning towards Joe.

'You must go back,' Ned said to Joe and Steve. 'You're not wanted for anything. You shouldn't get mixed up in this business.'

But they would not. They had their own reasons, as I learned that night, and they had their plans. Also they loved my brother. They loved him as much as men can love other men without it being the disgusting thing Aaron later sugges-

38

ted. I do not know what physical release men can find together, but I cannot believe it is the mockery Aaron made it out. Not that I think they loved like that – yet, maybe they did. They had all been in prison where they say such things are common, and they lived without women for long stretches. It horrified me when Aaron suggested it, but now I hope there *were* the times when they moaned away their need and their fear in each other's arms. Love is where you find it, and we cannot always be the ones to choose . . .

⌣

It was nearly night. Dan made damper, and Joe unwrapped fish that he and Steve had caught that morning. We ate and laughed and drank the whisky I had brought from home. Then we sat around the gold glowing mystery of the campfire, our cheeks hot and our arms, and our bodies chilled from the damp grass and the raw spring evening outside the circle of the flames.

The men talked and I lay propped up on their gear, watching them. They were half drunk, and I did not then take them seriously. They spoke of revolution, of the ideas of the men at Eureka twenty years before or more, of the unfairness of the law, the need to limit the power of property.

Joe was brought up on the gold diggings and he knew some of those who stood defiant against the Empire. My brother Edward was fervent in his agreement.

'It's not right,' he said loudly. 'It was the same in Ireland. The crown, which was not theirs, ruled them all. If you have no land, or if you have land but no wealth, you have no power either. We should rise up,' he said. 'We should take it from them, this power. What do you think, lads?'

They laughed and shouted and agreed, raucously. They spent the evening planning how to take down the men who had done them wrong.

'There are many who would follow us, too,' said Steve Hart. Of them all he was the most serious, then.

'It is a movement in the world,' he said, and spoke of France and Europe, which seemed very far away to us.

They planned it in detail as they had obviously done before – the Republic of North Eastern Victoria – but they did not mean it that night. They were not yet dying men grasping at straws. Not yet.

❧

I was given the hut. The men boasted of their hardiness out of doors, sleeping under the frosty stars in only their underwear, Edward naked to the waist. I chose my pallet carefully, trying to pick the one that Joe used, and lay down with my brother's coat and someone's rough blanket pulled around my ears. I did not sleep, I waited.

❧

He came later when the others were asleep, with his hand on his lips in case he startled me awake. I do not know the words to describe that first experience of love, and the memory is confused now, so much that is dreadful has come between. It was clumsy, awkward on my part; I had watched the animals on the farm but I did not realise how like a frog a person could become. It was warm. Rough and tender, but warm.

We lay curled up together in the old hut, staring at the clear pale sky through the chinks in the bark, talking and drowsing. I suppose Joe had come unthinking, following my scent as all animals do at these times, but now he must have realised it could be no light thing – not with Ned my brother and the man he was. So we talked of marriage. I was sixteen, my sister Maggie and my aunts had been married women by then. Joe thought his father would let us build a place on his property, to start.

'We'll have to wait,' I said. 'Until all this is over at least, and then until my mother is released.'

'Well, we will have to be careful, then,' he said, 'Little Kate.' And he stroked my jaw with his fine long fingers and kissed me, and this next time I got some pleasure too and began to learn what it might be like.

Before dawn he slid away, back to where the others were sleeping by the dead fire, and when I woke later the sun was high and warm. There was fresh damper on the rough log table and Ned and Steve had gone off to scout. I did not look at Joe but my body sensed his near all day, as it does when you are caught up in that madness of the flesh that we call love.

Dan was quiet, sulking. Perhaps he guessed my happiness and was baffled by it, perhaps it was only that he knew the end of his idyll was coming. It must have hurt him hard that he would lose his crop, his dreams – he kept insisting that the coppers might not find the camp, and if they did, well he could always come back later, when the hunt was off.

⌒

Ned and Steve came back at sundown. They had found the coppers' tracks, two sets of them. They had followed one lot back to the Old Shingle Hut, down-river from our camp.

'Jesus,' said Joe. He whistled softly. 'They are that close then?'

The other tracks left the river some miles up and went off into the trees. They had not followed those far, the cover there was too convenient for the police to ambush from.

'What are we going to do?' Somehow Dan was shaking off his sullen mood. He did not want to risk arrest again, but the prospect of action cheered him, although his mouth stayed tense with discontent.

'We will wait until morning and then bail them up,' said Ned. 'They have revolvers, but we can take their guns and tie

41

them up, make fools of them. By God, if Strahan is there I'll dare him to shoot me like a dog.'

Perhaps he had thoughts of a duel in the clearing beside the river – I do not know. There were the tracks of four men at the old hut, they said, but perhaps they did not realise which four men it was. This time it was not the cowards and the fools that had been sent out but some of their tough, brave men, who would not brag about what they hoped to do to Ned Kelly, but would try seriously to take him, and if not, then to kill him. Again Ned told Joe and Steve to go but they refused, even when he asked them to see me home. Finally, they agreed it was not safe for me to try and get away either. I could stay another night and slip off in the morning when they bailed the coppers up.

We sat again by the fire, breathing deeply the eucalyptus scented smoke, talking idly of ideas and government, taking it in turns to stand lookout in case any of the police had the sense to try to creep up on our camp at night. I suppose my excuse now is that I was half drowned by my body's ebb and flow, drugged almost to insensibility by the rising juices of my desire. But the men, too, seemed unconcerned. 'If only' is a destructive phrase, God knows, but it has drummed in my head always since that night. If they had escaped then in the night, across the border, if I had insisted that Joe and Steve see me home, if we had only known . . .

Joe came again to my hut and left early. The two nights blur into one in my memory, leaving impressions only of his lean young flesh, easily confused with later memories when we loved often: the slipperiness of loving bodies and yet the way they cling and cleave, the mysteries in what is in fact so commonplace.

⌒

I arrived afterwards because I was the lookout while the others crept to the Old Shingle Hut, and so I do not really know what went on before, only what my brothers and Joe told me later; and now, as then, I must believe them.

We had watched the police camp most of the day, one or another of us, reporting back as we changed watch, at intervals of an hour sometimes, so that our impressions of their activities were disjointed.

❧

A trooper built up the fire and went into the hut for provisions. He was young, not bad looking for a copper, he could have been a young family man – his wife would love him perhaps for his soft firm voice. He brought out flour and a basin and began to knead dough. His movements were careful, precise as a cat's. He looked up at a faint 'cooee' from the river bank. Another copper came into view – it was that Lonigan who had humiliated Edward in a fight the year before. They spoke softly, briefly, then both looked around. They could not see me deep inside the golden waving shadows. Lonigan sat down on a log and began to read a book he took from his pocket. I backed carefully, silently away from them.

❧

Dan said, 'There are two of them at the camp. I tried to see inside the hut in case the others are skulking there, but I couldn't. They might be out looking for us. They look peaceful.' His voice was wistful. Like me, he forgot to tell Ned it was Lonigan at the campfire; perhaps Dan did not know him by sight.

❧

Bread turned brown in the ashes; the smell merged with the earth and mimosa fragrances enclosing me. It was my turn again to watch. Lonigan was not there now. He must have gone back inside the hut, for a sleep perhaps. The other copper

43

stirred the fire idly with a stick, letting it burn and char and, when it shortened too much, bending to pick up another one, throwing the last into the coals. He seemed lulled, as I was, by the stillness of the bush at midday. I could not believe that he meant to harm us. I crept carefully away over faintly crackling twigs.

∽

'Where are the other two?' Edward was anxious. He knew there were the tracks of four men, but he did not know which were coming or going. 'Perhaps it is a trick and they're waiting inside the hut for us to make a move. But how can they know we have found them?'

He did not go himself to spy on their camp. He kept watch for the others returning. His ears were the keenest of us all – he boasted he could hear a leaf fall at a hundred paces.

∽

Joe slid clumsily, panting, into the clearing. He had dry leaves in his fair hair.

'They're eating,' he said. 'There are still only the two of them. By Jesus they're cool enough. You'd think they were on a bloody church picnic.'

We laughed, all of us, our tension drifting lightly into the green air. I wanted only to pick the tangles from his hair.

∽

'We are wasting time,' said my brother Edward. 'If the others are out scouting they'll come back before dark. We should move now while we can still surprise them.'

The four men moved off through the trees, their silhouettes blurred in the shifting sunlight. I was to follow at a distance and keep watch near the river for the other police. I looked at Joe, hoping for a gesture, a sign towards me, but he was too caught up in the excitement of the moment. I found a tree rising through dense shrubs and made myself a comfortable nest under it. Occasionally I could hear the soft whinny of the horses, hobbled further away in the trees. I hoped the coppers could not hear it too, or if they could that they thought it was their own.

After a long time I heard a shot. I froze. I had been told not to move from there whatever happened unless I saw the other police party.

What was I to do? What had happened? They had said nothing about shooting. Had the police crept up on them from the other direction? I did not know what to do so I obeyed my orders. Later – how much later I could not tell – I heard more shots. God, what was happening? Were they all dead? Joe with the twigs in his hair? My brothers? Steve? I would wait until dark, then I must find them. How would I tell Maggie? I waited, tense and cold with dread.

Just as I could stand it no longer and was about to move, Steve came creeping through the bush in the dusk. So they were not all killed then. He did not speak, only gestured for me to follow.

It should have been the death of all my hopes then, what I saw by the light of the fire and the dying sun in that clearing, but it would still take many months for the end to be complete, for the hunters to have their kill.

The blood stained everything, purple in the growing shadows, shockingly pink beside the fire in a last beam of sunlight where it trickled steadily from a policeman's chest. I did not see at first how many were dead and wounded, only the blood, and that Joe was alive. My brother Edward, bleeding from the face himself, was tying strips of cloth around Dan's shoulder. Two police lay near the camp. Lonigan, his face half smashed away, slumped over the log he had sat on to read that morning; the other, Scanlon, huddled in the dirt where he had fallen from his horse.

'Kate.' It was Steve Hart. 'Can you do anything for this poor bastard?'

I went over to the hurt man. They had torn away his jacket, and the wound glistened and pulsed under his arm. His face was white, but he did not groan, then, or later when he saw what they must do. I knew him, Sergeant Kennedy, married to Bridget Tobin not all that long ago. I looked at the blood.

'I don't know. Have you got something to wipe it with?'

Joe brought me rags and a basin of water from their hut, and I tried to clean the area of the wound. I could see in a few seconds it was no good. The blood would not stop and there was no place to bind or make a tourniquet. I stood up, almost fainting, me that had been brought up in the farmyard. I shook my head.

Ned came over to us and looked down at Kennedy.

'You were brave,' he said. 'I'll say that for you. Oh Jesus Christ why didn't you surrender as you were told?'

There was defeat and regret in Ned's face, his eyes deep muddy pools of bewilderment and sorrow. (The newspapers showed him at Stringybark Creek as a towering savage, teeth bared in triumph. But I was there, I saw him.)

'You have blood on your hands,' Ned said to me. 'You'd best go to the river and wash it off.'

For a moment I did not catch his meaning. Then I saw the way they were all standing, hands drooping over their guns, hangdog, and I realised. I looked at Kennedy lying there; he knew too.

'I'm sorry,' I said. 'There is nothing I can do for you.'

I stumbled down to the water, my sleeves catching on branches, tearing, my ankles twisting over the rutted ground. As I bent to splash my arms in the cold water I heard the last shot. I brought my hands dripping to my face and wiped, then shook off the droplets and went slowly back to the camp.

Edward dragged Kennedy's body off into the scrub. They gathered up the fallen revolvers and we stood looking around the clearing; it was too dark now to see the blood. Ned told Dan to catch the police horses as they would need spares if they hoped to get away.

'That bastard McIntyre,' Ned said. 'I trusted him to make them surrender.' He looked sadly at Scanlon's body. 'I did not mean to kill them, they compelled me to shoot them.'

He spoke to himself, yet it was as if he was already rehearsing his defence. McIntyre had escaped. We did not know that it would take him all night and most of the next day to report – that he must have panicked and got lost in the hills. We thought the police would be out hunting us by daybreak. I knew I could not go with the men – I did not even ask – but I waited silently while they packed up their gear at Dan's hut and stowed it over the saddles of the extra horses.

'Well, now we are all wanted,' Joe said with a laugh, but his mouth drew down, and he could not hide it. 'I will get back to see you Kate,' he said in a lower voice. 'Please tell my mother I will be all right.'

'Yes.' I said.

I stood for long after they had ridden off into the dark night, for long after I heard the last faint thud of the horses' hooves. Waiting, I suppose, but for what I do not know.

Finally I caught my horse, and because my bitterness was as great as Dan's I rode it again and again through his patch of beet, crushing the last of his dreamed fortune. Then I galloped home, not caring who heard or saw me in the long night, and of course no one did.

5

MY BROTHERS WOULD not go out of Victoria while my mother was still in prison, although we could have got them to Queensland easily enough. They hid up in the Warby Ranges at first and the marshes, and after in the Bogongs. Later, when they finally agreed to try and quit the country, it was too late.

We waited at home, while the days turned into weeks and the blood money went up from £500 to thousands of pounds for their arrest. Tommy Lloyd and Wild Wright rode into the hills every now and then and took provisions. They said the boys were pretty cheerful, and they were talking of robbing a bank or two to get enough money to hole up for years if they had to. And so they did. In December they held up the bank at Euroa, and a couple of months later, when the flood waters were down, they crossed into New South Wales and made their raid on Jerilderie.

It should have been only a time of fear and worry for us all, but the money from the bank robberies was welcome: Maggie and I had new clothes, and there were toys for the little ones and a new saddle for Gracie's mare. We did not see any of the gang, the money came through messengers. And it was easy to take simple pleasure in being flash for once and in laughing at the coppers who could not even stop our boys bailing up a police station. It was only later when the year began to turn cold and I was able to visit them in their caves, that I began to see the horror of it all.

◦

It was a morning when we played one of our tricks to deceive the police who surrounded the shack. We knew they were there – they had no more sense of hiding themselves than elephants. Sometimes we set the dogs on them for fun, but after they laid poison baits we had to keep the animals muzzled.

Maggie rode off fast with a couple of the dogs, and a rolled pack on her saddle behind her. They must have thought it was desperate for her to be taking provisions in broad daylight, and all the watching coppers jumped on their horses and followed her, galloping and crashing through the undergrowth. As soon as they were out of sight I loaded my own horse and cantered off quietly in the other direction. It was the first time I had been allowed to go to this camp – Ned had finally decided it was safe, since the coppers either could not see what was happening under their noses, or did not want to, the cowards that they were.

The autumn days were turning frosty, and I wore my new red wool jacket. I carried warm shirts for the men and blankets, and some salt beef from our grandmother Quinn in case they got snowed in.

By the time I got to the foothills it was dusk, and the mist had begun to roll down from the mountains, hiding the tops of the tall gums, until finally I could not see more than a few yards in front of me and had to dismount and walk beside the creeks, hoping that as I got higher the fog would thin. It is a thing I have always been afraid of, the fog, and the heavy dark shapes that loom out of it suddenly. My horse did not like it either, and he snorted and skittered as I led him under the branches. I began to think I had got lost and so was looking round for somewhere dry to curl up for the night when I heard Joe's call. I knew it was him, although it was only the sort of cooee we all used, larking around the place. I called back softly and waited for his shape to grow out of the drifting cloud. But his hand was on my arm before I saw him – they were all good at moving silently through the bush – and my body leapt as if my heart had fallen out.

'I've been waiting for you since noon, Kitty,' he said, and we stared at each other. His face was gaunt, his beard longer, but his eyes were fierce, and there was a sort of joy in his smile.

'I couldn't get away sooner. The coppers are all over the place.'

'I know. We see them sometimes, but they don't usually come up this far.' Joe took my horse's rein and led the way up the track to where his own horse waited. We had not yet embraced.

We spent the night in a lean-to not far from where he met me. Our bodies clung, and we kissed and kissed until it felt that we drained out of ourselves and into each other. Sometime in the night I woke and he was sitting by the bed watching me, a look of such tenderness on his face that I have never seen before or since on anyone. If I was not already melted that look would have destroyed me. He was dressed again.

'We'll have to go now,' he said. 'I didn't want to wake you, but we've a full day's ride.'

I got up and began to dress while he saddled the horses.

When I came outside he gave me a lump of hard tack to chew as we rode, and I got some of the sweet, withering red apples from my pack. We mounted, and just as we turned the horses he stopped me with a hand on my arm.

'Things at the camp . . .' He watched me.

'Yes?'

'They're not as good as they could be. Don't be too worried

by it. It is the cold and the loneliness. Not so many come up now that it's turning bad.'

I supposed he meant the weather, and perhaps he did.

❧

It was five months since I'd seen my brothers, and I could not hide my shock at their appearance. I had got used to Joe in the dark and the growing daylight, or perhaps I might have known earlier what to expect. They were so thin, burning up their energy in furious anxiety, and their eyes were wild, like Joe's. But Steve Hart was the worst. He sat dulled and shaking by the fire at the cave's entrance, a blanket around his shoulders, apart from the others.

Edward as usual had on only the lightest of clothing – breeches and a cotton shirt open to the waist – and Dan was hardly better, although he did wear a waistcoat and boots. Edward hugged me and kept me close to him, and even Dan seemed pleased that I had come, but they were all remote, as if I was an interesting visitor from another country, or as if they had crossed some frontier between them and their own flesh and blood. I wished I knew the words to bring them back.

Even Joe, through all our lovemaking of the next weeks, all our tender hoping and plotting, seemed, after that first night, already in another dimension.

They had nearly starved once, he told me, when the black trackers hired by the police had got too close, forcing them to retreat right up into the peaks of the mountains, not daring to try to shoot rabbits or the few birds at the snowline in case it brought the trackers to them. They lived on melted snow and roots and leaves, hoping they were not poisonous. When they came down again they found the camp undisturbed and no sign that the blacks had come anywhere near, but the horses had strayed and it took three days to round them up.

'Black devils,' Ned said. He admired them. They were the

51

only ones who ever beat him at reading the signs of the bush and they were the only ones he truly feared might find him.

I stayed until the snow began to fall lightly every day. I would have cheerfully been trapped there with them, but they would not hear of it. We had some good times, hunting rabbits and birds, fishing in the icy creeks, galloping across the valleys and boiling the billy at night over the flaming fire. Steve came somewhat to life and Joe said it was good for him to have me there. Steve had been arguing badly with the others, wanting to go back and give himself up. He was the least equipped for that hermit life at the mercies of the weather and every sudden noise. Unlike the others, he smelled, too, of neglect – stale sweat and even urine. He would not plunge into the freezing river as they did most days.

The others enjoyed it in a desperate way. In the end I think they were all relieved to see me go so that they could spring back into their hard, passionate struggle against the earth. Even Joe, although he held me so tight I could not breathe when he left me in the foothills, the tears running down his haggard cheeks. I think now that he fought a battle with what he thought was the soft side of his nature, and somewhere he was happy to be able to relinquish what I offered, though he did not say this. We made and remade our vows, crossing our fingers against the inevitable, always talking of 'When it is all over'. Well, I truly half believed still that soon it might be and that we might be together somewhere. Right up until the end I tried to cling to that hope, and perhaps it would have been better if I'd let it go then, into the mist and the swirling snow, as his form became shadow and disappeared.

6

ONE DAY Kate Byrne rode over to see me. I was surprised –
we had not had much to do with each other lately, my family
suspecting that Aaron was, in truth, working for the police.
After our awkward hellos she suggested that we walk down
by the river and have a talk.

As she walked she swished at the undergrowth with her
riding crop.

'Your mother has been over to see my mam,' she said
finally, stopping to stare back along the glistening grassy
banks. Where I stood I could see a small black spider with
yellow stripes and horns like the pictures of devils in sunday
school readers, absolutely still in its web, frightened I suppose
of such clumsy intruders. I did not know what Kate meant.
I thought it must have something to do with me and Joe and
wondered what my mother knew, or thought she knew. I
waited.

'She has told my mother that Aaron is a police spy.' The
way she stood, with her crop raised, I thought for a moment
she meant to strike me. But she let it fall and put out her other
hand to touch my arm. 'Oh, Kate, do you think he is, really?'

I was so relieved I did not see how much she could be hurt.

'Yes. Your own mother has seen him in the camp with them.' People thought I was hard then, when it was often only the covering up of my terrible secret softness.

'But . . .' Kate did not know what I knew, or how I thought of my own relations. 'But your own uncles have been giving them information – everybody does. It's a game they play, to mislead them. Isn't it?'

I began to see what I was doing to her, but I could not stop.

'We think that Aaron is giving them real information. My brothers have told him false plans and Aaron has passed them on, plans that they made him swear not to tell.' She was about to speak, to deny. 'It is your brother, too, up there. Hiding, trusting to the good faith of his friends.'

Her face closed. You may love someone more than your own family, but you may never admit it.

'My mother wants me to break with him. She says if I marry a man who betrays my brother I'll be cast out of the family forever.'

'She's right.' When you are young you are very certain of what is right and wrong; you do not fear the consequences because you can't imagine them.

'Yes. I suppose.'

We walked on, to where the bush came down right to the water and we could not pass in our long skirts and had to stop before we turned to go back. Her face was very sad, and her voice.

'You don't think . . . that things can become so confused that . . . you can lose your judgement . . .?'

'What do you mean?' I had no imagination then.

'Well, Aaron . . .' The tears ran, but her face was set and still. 'He might think he is acting for the best . . . It might not be – *deliberate*. D'you see?'

'No.' I only saw how they hated him, my brothers and Joe,

54

how they raved wild-eyed about how they would punish him. I wanted to share everything with them.

'Oh, well then,' she tried to smile, and her face went suddenly awry. 'If it is what everyone thinks, I suppose I had better get it over with.'

We walked back and when we came to our clearing she would not stop for tea but galloped off with her head high and her jaw clenched, straight to Aaron, I think, to tell him she did not want to associate any more with her brother's enemy.

◦

I went many times to the hideout in the hills, with provisions, or messages, or only to spend a few days with Joe, and each time the atmosphere at the camp was worse. I felt it then, but I did not take proper notice, being preoccupied with my love affair. And in any case I was used to the men in my family striding about with glaring eyes, ranting about one thing or another. Even though they had the threat of death over them I still could not take them that seriously.

They had stolen some parts of ploughs – the mouldboards – and beaten them over the fallen trunks of trees to make breastplates. Armour, Ned said, for when the police finally got off their arses and came for them. There was always liquor at the camp for they had another still set up, and Wild Wright and my Lloyd uncles brought them brandy whenever they visited. Dan and Steve were drunk most of the time, and Ned seemed sunk in listlessness, except when he and Joe argued about history and right and wrong. Joe seemed to smoulder those days, his eyes glowed and he could not stay still. He paced around the fire in the evenings, and when we went to bed he would not sleep. His lovemaking went on for hours – it was as if he could not finish, and it was an agony to him.

We lay in the firelight, wrapped in a blanket, and I watched him. With his eyes shut he looked like the heavy-lidded

55

saints in the old pictures that the priests were always showing us.

His eyes opened and he stared at me.

'What is it Kitty? What do you want?'

'Nothing. Go to sleep.' I smoothed the springy hair back from his forehead. Since I have had children I recognise that urge I had then to crush his face to my breast, to protect him from everything. Why did I not act? I was in limbo myself, holding to him, waiting on his decisions, like a mother letting him come to me. Perhaps I knew, somewhere, that I could do nothing.

In the end the men could not wait. They used the punishment of Aaron as an excuse, and Ned would not stop them. He tried to weave their revenge into his own dreams – Aaron's killing would make a diversion to draw up the troop train they knew was being sent to Glenrowan, and then they could make their final stand. The hours of planning, the interminable working out of details: what time Joe and Dan would shoot Aaron, how long it would take for the news to get to Melbourne, where they would derail the train, what speeches they would make as they disarmed the coppers and declared the new Republic. I listened and did not try to stop them. I thought they were right, that Aaron should be punished. He had said vile things and betrayed them for money. As for the rest – it seemed a game, nothing more. Everyone would be admiring, and somehow the price would be taken off their heads. I do not think I was stupid, only carried away, and bemused by all their endless talking. Even when Joe said he would shoot Aaron himself, like a lamed horse, I half-thought it could end in laughter or abuse or, at worst, fist-fighting. Women do not readily believe that men will face other men and pull the triggers of guns. I might even have egged him on. The Stringybark Creek episode was over a year before, and I had almost forgotten it.

❧

The day they killed Aaron, Joe and Dan came down to our place to visit, and to hide out until it was time. They did not tell us what they were going to do that evening, only that they had business in the district. I sat with Joe under the peppercorn tree and we held hands like any courting couple while Dan stayed inside with Maggie and watched her bake. He burnt his finger on the stove helping her get out the scones. He burnt his finger, and cursed, and put butter on the blister, saying 'Jesus, nothing hurts as bad as a burn, does it?'. And Maggie laughed and told him he was always a moaner and teased him about the big tough outlaw not being able to stand a little burn like that . . .

7

WHEN THEY CAME for us, Wild Wright and Tommy Lloyd, riding in the night like dogs out of hell, it was already too late. Maggie and I saddled our horses with trembling fingers in that grey time before dawn, while Gracie stood, yawning and terrified, but relieved to be ordered to stay at home with the little ones. They could hardly speak. I had never seen Wild Wright like that, his eyes blank with shock and something very like fear – not fear for his own safety, but fear at what had been set in motion and now could not be averted, at the fate he must have guessed was only hours away for his friends that he loved more than his own brother.

'The bastards.' His voice was slurred with spittle, and he had to swallow and hawk before he could make himself clear. 'We didn't think it would take the coppers so long to sound the alarm. They cowered like rats behind the women's skirts and didn't wire Melbourne until hours later.'

We had been told enough to fill in the details.

'Aaron . . .?' I said, but I already knew.

'Dead, and the coppers hiding in his house would not put in an appearance at all. Blast them and damn them to hell. They have beaten us by their own cowardly behaviour.'

The troop train had been much later arriving than the gang could have guessed, and by then their hostages at the Glenrowan hotel were restive, and they themselves were drunk and careless. The schoolmaster, Curnow, had run down the track and warned the train, and so there was no derailment and our men were taken by surprise before they could mount their ambush.

'It's like a bloody cattleyard,' Tommy Lloyd said. 'There is so much shrieking and rushing about and trampling, no one knows what the hell is going on.'

'Is anybody hurt?' They knew I meant any of ours.

Wild Wright put his hand on my arm. 'Joe was shot,' he said, and his grip tightened to hold me still. 'In the leg only, he was safe back inside the hotel when we left.' We galloped faster, I was so stiff with anxiety I could barely breathe, and my heart seemed to have stopped beating altogether. And yet it was to be worse than I could have feared, ever, in my most dreadful nightmares. Worse than anything I had thought could possibly be.

❧

When we got to the hotel at Glenrowan we could not push through the crowds of troopers and blustering men running about with guns and sticks. For more than an hour Maggie and I rode desperately to and fro around the edges of the fighting, trying to force our way nearer to the hotel, to our brothers and Joe. Men shouted to each other what was happening, and the bits of information we caught filled us with horror. It seemed at first that they were all dead, then later that some of them at least had escaped. Over and over we heard the cry, 'They've shot Ned Kelly!' or 'He's hit!'. Finally, we heard it so often we thought it could not be true. How could we have guessed that a man could be shot so many times and still survive?

Then, just as the sun came up in a bloody orange sunrise

59

there was a great shout, and this time we had to believe that Ned had been taken. Wild Wright came back from where he and his mates had been trying to break through the lines of people to bring my brother out, and his face was white and gaunt in the dirty light. He pushed a way for us, shouting 'Let them through! Let them pass! It's his sisters, damn your bloody hides!'.

Finally we were led by a shaking young policeman to the railway station where they had my brother laid out under heavy guard. The trooper helped us to dismount and took us inside. I was stiff with grief and shock and could not speak, but at the sight of Edward, torn and bleeding, Maggie let out a deep wail and began shouting incoherently at those around us. Ned was not conscious. Someone was attempting to bind his wounds; there were huge purpling bruises over most of his face. (We found later he had forgotten to put on the bala-clava Maggie had knitted to protect his head from the heavy helmet.)

He opened his eyes and looked at us with an exhausted smile. Maggie became silent as if someone had slapped her, and she went to his side, brushing aside the men who moved forward to block her way. She took his hand and knelt beside him on the dusty floor. I could not move or speak. I knew suddenly that Joe was dead – there was an empty place now where his life had flickered faintly inside mine, and I felt as cold as death. I heard what my brother whispered to Maggie, and for a moment I hated him.

'They would not come with me and fight out in the open. Why, Maggie? Why would they not come out and fight like men?' Maggie shook her head, the tears running like rain down her face. 'They must have taken their poison,' he said faintly. 'Why couldn't they wait to see it end? I had to watch it end.'

But Dan and Steve were not yet finished. A messenger came into the station-house and said someone who had escaped from the hotel reckoned the gang was still skulking in there, drinking and trying to give each other the courage to take their own lives. He told how Joe Byrne had died, too, wounded, drinking a toast to the Kelly Gang, shot again in the groin and dying in awful pain.

Maggie looked at me, and I nodded. At least he had not taken the coward's way out. I did not feel anything yet, only the cold empty place inside that will never now be filled again. I do not know how long I stood, frozen, by the wall. It must have been hours, because there was much coming and going around me, and Maggie was taken out to see if she could talk Dan into surrendering. She forced me to sit down on a bench as she went, and in answer to something she must have seen in my face, she said loudly, 'I will not tell a brother of mine to surrender. I will tell him to fight until his last breath.' And so of course they would not let her go into the hotel. It is just as well. In that mood she would have taken up a gun herself and stayed in there with them until the end.

The police forced us outside to watch the firing of the hotel in the afternoon, but by then I was past caring what happened. Maggie cried out and pulled against them, trying to run into the flames to save her baby brother, and they held onto her arms while she spat and clawed and shrieked. As the fire started another man ran out shouting 'The gang's all dead. For Christ's sake! There's still innocent people in there.' The priest and some volunteers ran in and came back dragging a couple of bodies. I could see that one of them was Joe, but I did not try to go to him as they hauled his corpse over to the stationhouse. It was later that they propped him up against the wall and took photographs for the newspapers – then I was taken away and knew nothing for days afterwards. I did not see them bring out the charred trunks of what had been Dan and Steve Hart; I lay in a cold fever, not aware even of the wake or the meetings of my brothers' friends in our house, planning a vengeance they all knew by now was not possible.

PART TWO

Interlude

THE TWO WOMEN sat in the railway carriage facing each other. One was young, hardly more than a girl, but with sadness in her face and a particular hard line beside her mouth. The other would also be young by some standards – if she had belonged to the wealthy classes and was pampered and rested – but she too was tired looking. When she worked she obviously worked hard.

They were both dressed well, in black, with wide-brimmed hats and gracious feathers, and their travelling jackets were made of good linen. They were not speaking. From the way the younger woman looked sometimes at her companion it seemed they had been arguing. At one point she leaned forward as if to touch the other on the knee, but something in the reflection she saw in the train window set her back, pressed against her seat, her eyes held to their own mirrors.

☙

Two men came in and sat beside the women, who shifted and stirred and smiled and sighed but still held their bitter looks for each other. That would wait. With the men came cool air from the passage and the smell of tobacco and whisky.

'You two aren't fighting still, are you?' The man speaking was the sort that always seemed to have a laugh behind his words, although he was large and tough-looking, not a person to antagonise lightly. He wore a big hat, like a drover's, and working-men's rough serge trousers, but his boots were freshly shined, and around his neck he wore a spotted scarf. Like his friend he had on a black armband.

The younger man might have been the women's brother. His bushy beard could not disguise the pointed Irish face and the easy wry mouth. He raised his eyebrow; he, too, was apparently a good-humoured man.

'Come on. You two must carry the whole burden now. There's no time for your squabbles.'

The younger woman looked at him. He was her favourite cousin, but he irritated her. He smiled his ingratiating smile, and she looked away.

The other man blew air through his closed lips in whispering puffs. He fidgeted, looked at the window, seeing only the doubled image of the carriage with its four people and polished wood. He scratched his thigh, brought out a pack of cards and flicked through them again and again. He did not like being confined in small rooms; he was a man who would always prefer a bucking, half-broken stallion, so that he could wave his hat in the air and shout. But there was something about the woman sitting beside him, the older of the two, which kept him still and fairly quiet. He looked at her from time to time but she stared out into a blackness interrupted only by the occasional gleam of the track or an infrequent lantern at some country station. Her soft pouting mouth was pursed, and there was a deep frown line between her heavy-lidded eyes. The words 'dark, bruised, Irish rose' came to his mind from somewhere – he was given to occasional poetic thoughts.

Across from him Tommy Lloyd slid down in his seat and let his hat tip forward, hiding his face. He held his hands across his stomach, shifting slightly to release his pants hitched into the crack of his behind, and gave a deep sigh.

'He can sleep anywhere, that boy. He has always been able to.' The younger woman's voice was affectionate, but also impatient.

The other man looked at her. He would be pleased to have someone to talk to.

'What will Jim do now, d'you think?'

She sighed and glanced at her sister, who from her posture was listening, but would not turn.

'I don't know. He's still full of remorse that he was not there with them. Though what good that might have done I don't know.' Her voice sharpened. 'Another corpse for them to gawk at, that's all.'

She looked the sort of person whose statements would always have a hidden edge, although her face was pale and soft. But there was a deep crease in the skin on one side of her mouth only, as if she were more used to the wry grimace than the full-lipped smile.

'I suppose he will come back eventually. If he doesn't get arrested again, that is.'

'He has done nothing.' Her sister's voice was deep, slow. She spoke almost automatically: it was something she had said often, about too many people.

'Not yet.' Kate's own voice was hard, but she was pleased that Maggie had finally spoken. 'There are some who grow to like prison, they say. Who set out deliberately to get put away again when they have only just got released.'

'He will not be arrested again.' Maggie was definite. 'They have finished with us now.'

'By God,' the man blustered. 'They had better be. I will shoot them all myself, like dogs, if they come near you again.'

'All this talk of shooting had better stop, too.' Maggie

turned back to her dark window, weary to death of the boasting men. In her lap she twisted the black band she had taken off her own arm. Her husband was coming out of prison soon. She wondered if Kate would stay around this time to help – they had been away from the farm for nearly three months, there would be a lot to do. She flicked her eyes quickly towards her sister, whose face had become animated with Wild Wright's defiant words. She would not settle easily to the farmwork after these years of almost being part of the gang. Riding frenziedly through the hills and the swamp, being shot at, a local heroine, sung about. And also, the older woman supposed, snatching the moments for her desperate love affair with Joe. For a moment she leaned towards the rough textures of Wild Wright; it had been a long time without Bill.

Maggie had had the adventures too, as much as Kate, but she was older, and there had always been something more settled in her nature. She felt nothing but relief now, mixed with the mourning, that it was over. She suspected Kate felt something else.

The picture of her sister strutting about on stage, performing clownish tricks on the pony – *Ned*'s pony – came into her mind, and hostility rushed through her again. Although it was weeks ago she could barely stop herself from slapping and screeching. Yet – she remembered the gouts of tears from Kate afterwards, and the awful moan that would not stop but went on and on like old women's keening, only worse, deeper, and with no tune at all.

'Oh Maggie, Maggie,' she had said. 'I can't take it, don't you see? I can't bear it at all. Why shouldn't I try to get something back from it, if it takes my mind off . . .' twisting her head away. 'And I like this – the clapping and the laughter. It makes me feel . . . somebody . . . as if I might live again . . .'

'But they are laughing at you, and at *him* too.'

'No, they're not. They are laughing with us. They are. They

hate the coppers and love the memory of Ned Kelly, they wouldn't laugh at him . . .'

Then had come the awful moan, which kept on and on, like a dingo calling at the moon, so that they had had to send for a doctor to give her laudanum, double or triple the normal dose.

Kate and Jim had taken the Kelly Show to Sydney after the Melbourne police closed it down, swearing they would make enough money to leave this rotten country. But even Sydney thought it in poor taste. The authorities were outraged by the larrikin element of the audiences, and they had to close there, too, after only a few days.

Now . . . there was something wild about her, Maggie thought suddenly, and she was frightened. She remembered how Kate was before they killed poor fumbling Aaron.

'He has insulted us and betrayed us,' Kate had said. Then, in a shocked whisper, her eyes glittering, 'He said he would shoot Joe dead and then . . .' her voice dropped even lower, 'and then . . . fuck him. In his arse. He said that's what they were all doing up in the hills anyway, with each other. That they were not true men at all but liked to dress in women's clothes and pretend to be sweethearts. So,' her voice had become cold and certain, 'Joe says he must be punished. Also, it's part of the plan.'

Well, the plan went wrong, as Maggie had known it would. She had told Ned not to let them shoot Aaron. 'You are putting yourselves on the other side then,' she had said. 'If you kill him in cold blood there will be no one willing to make excuses for you.'

But by then Ned could not command Joe and Dan. 'They will do it anyway,' he had said, and shrugged. The months in the swamps had transformed his body, emaciating it to a point of pale hardness. 'Anyway, it will do as a decoy, to make sure they bring up the troop train in time.'

He was wrong. They were all wrong. And she had been right. But that was no comfort at all, and there were many nights ahead to rediscover that. She shuddered, and the man beside her picked up her shawl from the seat and wrapped it around her shoulders.

She looked at her cousin slumped on his seat.

'I think I will try to sleep, too,' she said to Wild Wright. She closed her eyes and her face relaxed. Her hair shone thickly, untidy from the hat now in her lap.

Wild Wright laughed and got up.

'Well, I can't rest on these bloody things. I think I'll stretch my legs a bit.' He was talking to Kate, but she too, had her eyes shut. She looked gentle, innocent, younger than eighteen.

But he stopped at the carriage door and looked back. Kate's eyes were open and she was staring, staring, at the black marching night . . .

1

Greta

PEOPLE DID NOT ride off the road now to the Widow Kelly's. Those who did at first, in the days just after she was released, to say hello and give their best, had been quickly discouraged by the solemn, wizened little woman.

'There is no whisky here any more,' she would say, and they would be lucky to get past the gate where she stood, usually with a young child hanging on her skirt, the dogs nearby pulling eagerly on their chains. Even those who had helped the boys and claimed they were part of the uprising (if only Ned had given the signal – they could show their armour to prove it), even they were given a cold look or a neutral half-believing smile and sent on their way without so much as a mug of water.

The girls, too, as wild as they had been, it was hard to credit them now. Maggie – well she was older, more like her mother. But young Kate, the spirited one people sang songs about, you'd never have thought she'd turn so blank and hostile. People were disappointed. It seemed, finally, that it was all over. Even Jim, the only one left of the three Kelly boys, had reformed. He never left the property now – he was likely to go off quietly and shut himself in the hut when you tried to visit, rather than stop to yarn a bit about the old days.

But people had seen one of the girls at least, off in the hills past Greta where the gang had had its hideout, trotting quietly on her brown horse, stopping now and then for no obvious reason, almost as though she were looking for something, or someone. Kate probably, waiting for her brother's ghost. But somehow people didn't snigger. It was a terrible thing after all.

❧

It was usually after a row with her mother or Maggie that Kate saddled the horse and rode off into the bush. If she was very angry she would not bother with the saddle, but sat astride, her bare heels digging into the horse's flanks, lying low on his back under the small trees along the river bank, pushing him faster and faster through the scrub, around and over the tangled undergrowth and the old, rotting logs.

Maggie, wiping her hands on her old apron, watched her go. The good clothes were put away – it had been a brief period of being the fashionable Mrs Skillion. There was still strain between them from Kate's behaviour in Melbourne, although Maggie had defended her to their mother when she heard of it, just out of jail, the reporters crowding round the frail old woman asking what she'd thought of her daughter's tasteless performance, 'In the very shadow of the gallows'.

Mrs Kelly came out of the house and watched Kate too. Her face was wrinkled and drawn now, she had become thin in prison, a little twig of a woman, but her back was still stiff, and her dark sunken eyes could stare down any man.

'Well?' she said to her eldest daughter. 'What will become of her I wonder?'

'Oh,' Maggie forced the worried frown off her own face. 'She'll settle, I think. She has more to get over than us, after

72

all – Joe too, and the pictures they took of him after to remind her.'

'Wild animals!' The old woman spat into the dust. 'To prop up a corpse and take bloody photographs. It was enough to turn her brain completely.' Her hand lifted in an old, almost forgotten gesture, as if she meant to cross herself against what she had said. 'Well, I better get back to the bread or we will have no dinner.' At the door she turned back. 'Why don't you go after her, Maggie? Try to make it up? It can't last, all this anger between you – she only wants you to forgive her.'

'Yes.' Maggie would have liked to forgive her sister. 'All right. I will.' She saddled her own mare, pulling each strap tight, feeling with careful fingers under the horse's belly as she dragged in the girth. She mounted and rode off slowly, sedately side-saddle for once, the horse high-stepping down the rutted back.

Gracie ran out after her, calling.

'Here, some food.' She was breathless. 'Mum said.'

Maggie took the parcel. Well, perhaps they could have a friendly picnic. Why not? If she could find her.

But it was not difficult. Kate's horse was roped to a stump at the place where the river divided marshy flats on one side and the foothills of the ranges on the other. Where the swamps began the trees were smaller, stunted by the rich prickly scrub that spread around them. The hills rose on the other side and so did the timber, white pure trunks of gum-trees, and under them the green and golden shadows like the feathers of a small parrot ruffling in the breeze.

Maggie tied her own horse and went carefully through the sharp shrubs until, bending aside a spiky branch, she saw her sister. She put her hand to her mouth and was still, watching.

Kate stood against, leaning into, the trunk of a tall sapling. Her arms were around it, the length of her body pressed to its slender column. With her eyes closed she was kissing the smooth, creamy bark, her neck exposed, stretching, her mouth wide open, drinking in the kiss so that Maggie could see her tongue moving.

Kate heard something – Maggie's sharp drawn breath, or the crackle of the twigs – and slowly opened her eyes. Without taking her arms from around the tree she leant outwards, langorously. 'Oh, it's you.' Her voice was low and disappointed. She withdrew her body reluctantly, as if it were the tree that clung, and she shrugged, her hand wafting upwards.

'What do you want? Why won't you leave me alone?'

'Oh Kitty.' Maggie wanted to hold out her arms but did not. 'I've brought some bread and cheese – can't we sit down somewhere and talk? *She*,' she gestured towards their house, 'our mother, is very upset, and so am I. It can't go on like this.'

'I say that every minute and every hour of every day, but it seems that it can.' The confused softness in Kate's face hardened, the small line beside her mouth became deeper, perhaps she would finally cry. But she smiled instead, mocking. 'I know, I am hard to put up with. I don't know what to do with myself, either.'

She turned away, then back. Maggie spread the teacloth, and they sat on a fallen log to eat the thick sandwiches. For a while they did not speak. Maggie was afraid that what she would say would not be the helpful thing she had come to offer, and Kate brooded, her eyes sliding off, unfocused, as if some tender, throbbing area of her brain troubled her, something nagging and jagged under whatever else she was doing or saying.

'I am sorry for the things I said to you in Melbourne,' Maggie said, 'when we picked you up.' She gave a heavy sigh. It was hard to renounce justified resentment. 'I know you were distraught and people took advantage of you.'

'Yes, perhaps,' Kate said softly. She crumbled her crusts and threw them on the ground as if they were at home and she expected the hens to come clucking round her for the scraps. For a moment she sat stiff and still; then, and it seemed almost

74

an act of her own kindness, she suddenly gave in, and burying her face in her sister's soft breast, began to cry. Her sobs at first were so loud and unrestrained that Maggie was afraid she would lose control again, completely, with no one around this time to help hold her down or keep her from hurting herself in the wild thrashing about of her limbs. But gradually Kate quietened and lay relaxed against her while Maggie stroked the hair off her forehead, again and again, smoothing each escaped tendril back to the hard shape of the skull beneath.

After a while she said 'Are you awake?'

'Yes.' Kate sat up, her face puffed, sensual from the tears. 'Oh Jesus,' she tried with her hands to smooth her crumpled face, pulling her cheeks down until her mouth gaped and her eyes showed red-veined rims.

'Careful that the wind doesn't change,' Maggie said. They gave each other resigned, tight smiles and Maggie shook out the cloth.

Then they rode home fast, shouting to each other, trivial things about the river and the new hut on Bricky's land, until they came to the track that led to their own place. Then Kate called, 'Race you!' and galloped ahead, bent over her horse like a jockey, stooping once, quickly, to the ground to pick up a rock – showing off, Maggie thought affectionately. But it niggled at her that she had been the only one to apologise.

2
Adelaide

AFTER THAT Kate still rode to the hills and sat, straight-backed and stiff on her horse, staring at the dark hollows of the valleys, trying to make out the old tracks, searching the mountains for landmarks – an old, twisted white trunk, or the bald, grassless patch under tall trees – staring until her eyes ached or watered. Then she would suddenly wheel about and gallop down through the foothills as fast as the horse would go, surefooted, never stumbling, whipping through the scrub and splashing across the creek, home.

⟳

One day a man rode up to the gate and dismounted. Gracie was outside tending to the animals so she set down her buckets and went to see what he wanted. She was used to putting off those who wanted to see her mother or her brother, Jim.

The stranger was a tall man, sandy and weather-burnt. He twisted his hat in his hands, squinting at the girl.

'Miss Kate Kelly?' It was a nervous question. He had to clear his throat in the middle of asking.

'I'm Grace,' she said, sharply.

76

'No. That is, I didn't mean were you her. I know her, Miss Kelly that is . . .' He looked up the road he had ridden, perhaps wishing himself back along it. He hawked in his throat again.

'I met yer sister in Sydney,' he said, rushing now, almost bold. 'She kindly said to call in should I ever be passing.'

'Oh. You want Kate?' Gracie was uncertain. She looked towards the house. 'Well,' she said, and stared hard at his face, trying to appraise him. 'Well. I don't know, really . . . I suppose . . .'

Although her voice was hardly welcoming she unhooked the gate and leant on it, swinging, until he was through. He didn't wait for her to fasten the chain but slipped his reins over the post and walked straight to the door and knocked. Gracie picked up her buckets and stood watching him.

Her mother opened the door and gave the girl a surprised glare. Then Kate came too, and peering over their mother's shoulder, seemed to smile. The women stood back and the man went past them into the dim house. Gracie hefted the buckets thoughtfully and walked back to the shed to refill them.

❧

They were in Adelaide three weeks before Kate began to get restless. The ginger, peeling man talked of marrying her, but with a certain shiftiness which she suspected hid another wife somewhere. When they had first met in Sydney, he had told her he had his own business, but he now turned out to be little more than a tinker, driving his dray out into the little townships in the hills, selling cloth and pins and patent medicines off the cart.

She started going with him on his trips. It was peaceful driving along the uneven tracks, jolting under the weak winter sun, and the foothills reminded her of home, which for a while was acceptable. He let her drive the dray back sometimes but he would not promise to buy her another horse for riding. The fine brown mare he had had in Sydney turned out to be hired, like the tall stallion he rode to the Kellys' house to fetch her. She had sold her own horse in Melbourne on their way through.

They spent their nights in a small hotel near the railway station when they were in town. He had a shack in the bush, he told her, but he was evasive about taking her there just yet. He earned little money and was mean with that, expecting her to pay for her own meals and the bits and pieces of clothing she needed. Gradually the talk of marriage ceased, and his conversation turned to ways she could earn her own keep.

'You could be a barmaid,' he said one night, looking at her admiringly as she lay half undressed on the lumpy bed.

'The hotel here needs staff, the manager told me only yesterday.' She knew he had not spoken to the manager but had probably got the information from the kitchen skivvy, who was a relative of his. She said nothing, but she had already decided to leave him. She was inclined to think of going on the stage. Her time in Sydney, with crowds following her as she rode with Jim along the water's edge at Woolloomooloo, the cheers and redfaced admiration after the shows, had stayed with her, the only painless memory.

The next day when he rode out she stayed in bed, telling him she had women's troubles. He left her a bottle of the remedy he kept for the tired-looking wives at remote homesteads – a mixture heavily based on laudanum, ensuring repeated and regular sales – and went, with some relief, alone. The trip would take two or three days, and there was a widow, a cook at a large farmhouse along the way, in whose placid eye he thought he had surprised a flash of jealousy last time through, at Kate sitting up in the cart beside him.

It had been an annoying trip, that one, Kate complaining all the time – at the small tent he pitched beside the dray at night, and about the cold, hard ground under the thick blankets, sitting hunched up and resentful all the way back to town.

He spat over the side of the cart as he drove out. Perhaps he would call in at the old place on the way back – one thing, that lazy bitch never complained if he lost his temper or knocked her about a bit. This one, he spat again. This one back at the hotel, she was a real disappointment. Bloody putting on airs, and her the sister of a murderer, too. When he'd met her in Sydney he'd thought she had a bit of go to her, he'd been flattered that the flashy Kate Kelly had gone about with him. But now ... All she did was lie around the hotel, refusing to get work, complaining and nagging, and the one time he'd raised his fist to her to shut her up, be buggered if she didn't rush out and come back with a bloody great knife. That's what she needed, though, a decent slap around the ears. That'd show her what was what. The pleasure that this thought gave him as he jostled his way towards the compliant widow was already irrelevant, as by the time he reached Adelaide again Kate would have disappeared, having changed her name, and he would not knowingly set eyes on her again.

3

Elsie

THE DRESSING-ROOM where the small group of women shivered and waited was cramped and smelled of sweat and stale perfume. The fat, over-rouged woman sitting on the only chair suddenly turned to Kate.

'Hey,' she said, loudly, but not unkindly, 'Hey. What's yer name?'

'Ada.' It came automatically now after the weeks of trooping through the theatre managers' offices. 'Ada Hennessey.' A high-class name she thought. She had never known anyone called Ada – she had seen the name in a newspaper, referring to some relative of royalty, and Hennessey was a name off one of the sandy man's patent medicine jars.

'Yer done much dancing love?' The woman appeared to be chewing something, she rolled her tongue to the side of her mouth before speaking. When Kate came to know her better she realised the woman was never without her little bag of lozenges – sugary, red things, which she claimed were medicinal and kept her energetic.

'A little bit.' Then, more truthfully, 'Not much. But I think I could learn.'

'You got good legs anyway.' The women were undressed down to their shifts and stockings. 'That's the main thing.' The fat woman sighed, as if regretting her own lost slimness.

'Go on, Elsie,' a thin, spiteful-looking woman said. 'Youse never had to worry about the shape of your legs – just who yer wrapped them round.' The other women sniggered.

'I suppose you want to be an actress too, do yer?'

The thin woman peered at Kate.

'Course she does,' said Elsie protectively. 'And why shouldn't she? Some people are luckier than others, after all.'

'Heh.' The thin woman seemed to change her mind about spitting, but she was contemptuous. 'None of us's ever been lucky,' she said, 'And this one don't look it either.'

It was Kate's own opinion now, too. She decided this would be her last try-out, she was sick of beery men feeling her calves as if she was a bloody horse. She made a wry face, causing the thin woman to back down.

'Never mind dearie.' What had seemed to be spitefulness in her face was simply crudely applied make-up, Kate now saw. The eyes, inside their hard black lines, were watery and weak, the mouth much fuller than the hard red cupid's bow allowed.

'Youse might be the one in a million who gets on, you never know. Me,' she sighed and looked around. 'Me, I'm going to give it up if I don't get a part in this show. I'm too bloody old to be freezing me bum off in these rabbit hutches.'

'You're too bloody old for anything, Ivy, why don't you face it and give us all a rest?' It was a small fair girl speaking. Unlike the others, she had on a dancer's frilled petticoat and her black stockings looked like silk. Also unlike the others, she stood up straight and confident, not slouching against the wall or hunched up on the dressing tables.

'She's bedding with the manager, that's why she's so chirpy,' Elsie whispered loudly in Kate's ear. The girl ignored her.

A starved looking youth appeared at the door.

'Gawd,' he said with a marked cockney accent. 'We want

81

some cheerful looking girls for this, not a bunch of miserable hags like you lot.'

'Piss off yer little bastard,' Ivy said calmly.

'Well, come on then,' the boy said. 'Let's have yer. Get up on the stage and do yer stuff.' He winked at the fair girl, and she smiled.

'Bloody suckup,' Elsie muttered.

They filed out into the theatre where the manager was sitting waiting.

'All right girls,' he said when he saw them. 'Now this is a new little number like they're doing in Paris, France.' He got up and came over to them. 'You'll have to wear petticoats like the one Rose's got on here,' he put his hand possessively on the fair girl's behind.

'And then you'll have to kick up your legs a bit, like this.' He did a few crude, kicking steps, lifting an imaginary skirt to show his legs as far as the place a garter would be.

'All right Joey,' he shouted, and the cockney boy came in and sat at the piano. He played a few notes of a fast polka, and the women sorted themselves into a rough, wavering line on the stage. Most of them had seen the French dancers at the interval of the circus and had a general idea of what was wanted.

The boy played, and the women kicked their legs. After a few minutes Elsie dropped out of the line and went to sit beside the manager. 'Too old,' she wheezed. 'Too fat for all this goings on.'

'Never mind, Else,' the manager comforted her. 'You can sell the fruit and nuts out front like you always do.'

She sat back with a satisfied smile, it was what she'd come for. Most of these old managers knew her from the days she'd ridden horses around the ring bareback, wearing only a brief dress of spangles and tulle, and they'd usually give her some small job that carried good tips and the chance for some lucrative whoring on the side.

'That new one looks all right,' she said, pointing at Kate.

He grunted. 'Hmm. Her timing's bad.'

When the boy finished playing the women stood, panting, their hands on their hips, watching the manager. He got up slowly and came to the edge of the stage.

'You. And you, and you.' He went through the line, pointing first at the girl called Rose, then at four or five others. He did not choose Kate, although he looked appreciatively at her legs as he passed.

While the lucky ones stayed on stage to dance again for him to pick the front line, Kate went with the others, including Ivy, back to the dressing-room. When she was dressed she found Ivy and Elsie waiting for her outside.

'We thought yer looked pale, dearie,' Elsie explained. 'You can come back to my place for a cup of tea if you like.'

❧

Weeks later, when it was over, Elsie said she and Ivy had known the minute they saw her.

'I said to Ive when we was getting dressed,' she said. 'You know, after that audition for old Fred Harris. I said "If that girl's not got a bun in the oven I'm not Elsie Green."'

'But I didn't know myself, then.' Although she should have realised the unaccustomed lethargy and passive trailing about of those weeks had some cause.

She was still weak after the visit to the old woman Ivy knew who lived in a shack behind the railway. There had been fever, and she had lost a lot of blood. But it was not the operation, ghastly and sordid as it had been, that had most shocked her, but her revulsion at the thought of that pale-eyed man's child inside her body, contaminating her from the innards out, like a giant slug growing there.

'He was so . . . sandy.' She tried to explain to Elsie.

'Oh women often feel like that,' Elsie said. 'You're sick at the thought of it for a few weeks, then you seem to get used to it.'

Elsie was worried about her and about what she had let out during her illness, that she and Ivy never talked about, except to tell her that she had said her name was Kate.

'Ada Hennessey was just my stage name,' she said, and they were glad to accept it. 'Kate Ambrose is my real name.'

Elsie and Ivy listened and did not mention the ravings about guns and coppers, one brother left burning and the other dancing at the end of a rope.

～

Kate liked the little room she had at the top of the lodging-house. Elsie and Ivy were away at work in the late afternoons and evenings, Elsie selling fruit at the theatre and sometimes going off with men afterwards for pocket-money and Ivy working as a barmaid and cleaner at the hotel on the corner.

She lay, in the weeks after her fever dropped, drowsing, and watching the sunlight and shadows passing across the wall, tinted blue and red by the little panes of stained glass at the corners of her window. In the mornings Elsie would come in, with oranges and milk or a fresh bun from the bakers if she had returned late enough the night before to pass them loading the dray. She brought the newspaper and, her lozenges tongued to the side of her mouth, read Kate the juicy items as she lay propped up against her pillows, sipping her warm milk.

Ivy would come in later, briefly, to see if Kate wanted anything or to help her to the washbasin.

'I don't like sick-rooms, and that's a fact,' she said apologetically, her eyes frightened inside their black rims. Yet it was she who had emptied Kate's slops and the chamber-pot during the worst of it.

When Ivy came, she was fighting a headache, usually from the night's drinking. She appeared at the door with a glass of stout in her hand, gulping down Holloway's pills with each mouthful.

'It'll be the death of me, working in a bloody pub,' she said, not meaning it. 'Like giving a thief a job at the bank.'

But Kate could see already that it was affecting her. Each day the black lines seemed less to contain the eyes than to be seeping from them, and the deep scarlet mouth spread outwards, radiating, by the end of the night, into the deep wrinkles around her lips.

Elsie was worried. 'She's always liked the bottle,' she said. 'Like the rest of us. But now – she gets treated all night, and she takes the leftovers. She's never bloody sober.'

Gradually Kate was well enough to get up and sit in a wicker chair on her little balcony in the warm spring sunlight, watching the people and the traffic in the street below.

Although her strength was returning fast she found it hard to believe she would ever be robust enough to walk briskly down the pavement like the women she saw in the street, or press her legs strongly against a horse's flanks to control it. She half lay on cushions, watching the coaches and drays pulling up at the shops and houses across the street, feeling very far removed from the bustle of other people's lives, not even wanting to be part of it herself again. But she had no money left and owed some to Elsie, who had cheerfully paid for her food and the next month's rent.

Even as she thought she could sit forever lazily in the sunshine, her bones melting in the golden heat, she knew she would soon have to get a job. If she was rich, she thought, she would do nothing all day except lie propped up on pillows with servants to bring her food and drink and bathe her and brush her hair and wrap soft clothes around her.

She went with Ivy to see the publican at the corner. He was a small neat man and Ivy fawned on him, her eyes shifting nervously as she introduced them; she was afraid he had noticed her own inefficiency.

'Have you ever worked in a hotel before, Miss Hennessey?' He spoke carefully, as if he had at some time gone to a lot of trouble to correct any mistakes of grammar or pronunciation.

'Well, not really. But I cooked and kept house for my family always, while they worked the farm.' She hoped he would not think her too frail for the hours of standing behind a bar.

He looked at her thoughtfully. 'Well . . .' He was a man who liked to have others hanging on his decisions, and this girl, with her wide anxious eyes, had his approval.

'Well, at first I'll put you on half wages, while you're learning. Then we'll see. Mrs Grote here will teach you all she knows, won't you Ivy?'

Ivy rustled with relief at Kate's success, and pleasure at being so familiarly addressed. Her voice, coarser than it used to be, croaked its satisfaction.

'Oh, I'm sure she's a willing worker, Mr Scott. She'll soon be pulling ale with the best of us.'

'Yes. Well, not too soon. I want you to learn everything properly. I can't abide sloppy barmaids, it puts the customers off.'

Did his malicious little eyes rest on Ivy? Her ludicrous red mouth turned down instantly like a clown's.

'All right then,' he said, dismissing them. 'You can start today. Come in time to clean up before the evening meal.' He rubbed his hands on his shiny black cuffs in satisfaction. If she didn't work out he'd soon find another one to train. It would save him money in the long run.

The two women said goodbye at the door of the hotel. Ivy had to begin cleaning the saloon bar for the afternoon drinkers.

'How long will it be before he pays me my proper wage?'

'Oh,' Ivy looked around shiftily. She was not paid the full rate herself, which was why she had got the job.

'A couple of weeks probably, and you'll get your tips, too, don't forget.' She cackled suddenly. 'And yer drinks as well – he can't see what you carry off in your stomach, can he now?' Her white powdery face wobbled in the doorway. 'They're calling me, love. I'll see you later on.'

She shut the door, and Kate walked slowly back to her room. It would have to do. At least until she was stronger and had the energy to look for something better.

For the next few months the rhythms of the hotel took over. After a couple of weeks, when he had seen that she could answer back and was not intimidated by the rough men gazing at her low bodice, William Scott had increased her wage to nearly the proper level. She was expected to help make up the rooms and wash the dishes in the kitchen as well as tend the bar and serve in the dining-room on his wife's days off. But Kate was happy. The only thing marring her tired contented routine was the now hurtling deterioration of Ivy. In the hotel Kate tried to cover for her, although late in the evening when the bar was full and the guests were also ordering their drinks from the verandah, this was almost impossible.

One night, after work, Kate found her crumpled against a wall between the hotel and their rooms, her skirt still hitched around her waist and her hand closed tightly around the coins left by her hasty customer. But most nights now, Ivy was too far gone even for these still profitable expeditions, and Kate would stagger home with her, heaving the half-conscious older woman along under her arm like a huge, dragging doll.

Scott said nothing, but he watched from his office across the corridor from the bar, and sometimes Kate thought she saw him looking from the half-lighted doorway as she and Ivy stumbled home.

One day he came out as Kate arrived and called her into

his little cubby-hole. She stood by the door, wondering if he had noticed the small bundles of leftover food she took home after the lunch hour, but when he turned from peering through his dusty window she saw that he was smiling.

'You're shaping up well, lassie,' he said. 'And Mrs Scott says you're a willing helper in the kitchen, too. You'll be a first-class barmaid soon, I'll guarantee you.'

She relaxed. 'Thank you.'

'Well, I'm a fair man, and I like to reward honest effort when I see it, so I've decided to increase your salary.' His small hard eyes twinkled at her. 'You'll be getting the same as the others, with ten years experience, from now on. And I'll expect you to be grateful and repay me by always working hard.'

Kate told Ivy as they walked back to the lodging-house for lunch. Ivy sniffed loudly, she was already half drunk, and her mouth was blotched red in one corner as if clumsily kissed.

'There must be something he's got in mind,' she said, her voice slurred with suspicion. 'P'raps he's got his eye on you, eh?'

They both laughed. It was impossible to think of that man, with his fastidious little mouth, having his eye on anyone.

After the evening work was finished they found out what it was all about. As he handed over their wages William Scott asked Ivy, in a curt voice, to stay a minute. She smiled, fuddled, vaguely nodding as Kate whispered she'd wait outside.

In a few minutes Ivy staggered out, hiccoughing and sob-bing, blindly struggling past Kate who had to hurry after her. Scott had given Ivy the sack, telling her she was lucky he didn't prosecute for all the liquor she'd stolen, and the way she'd turned his hotel into a place of evil repute with her lewd goings-on.

Elsie wasn't surprised when Kate waited up to tell her.

'That'd be why he's upped your money,' she said, her fat face hard and knowing, her throat moving up and down, vici-ously chewing. 'He's worked out that you're doing Ivy's work as well, anyway, so why pay the two of you? That's probably what he had in mind all along, getting someone who'd take over from the poor old bugger.'

On Elsie's advice Kate said nothing to Scott, but she no longer bothered to be friendly to him at work. Jobs were too hard to get, Elsie said, to get hoity-toity about that bastard, and anyway it wouldn't do Ivy any good – he wouldn't give her her job back whatever Kate did.

But although Ivy hadn't been much help for a while, the job was much harder with her gone, and Kate's days now began early and finished late. Some days she didn't have the time to go back to her little room for lunch, but had to eat at the hotel from whatever scraps the cook could make up for her. Weeks went by when she hardly ever saw Elsie or Ivy, except sometimes in the early mornings if she was up when Elsie came home from an after-theatre 'visit'.

One morning they sat on Kate's balcony, drinking beer and eating buttered toast, and they saw Ivy making her uncertain way up the street below them, zigzagging across the sidewalk, propelling herself along by pushing at the walls with each inward lurch, then careering out again a few feet into the passers by, and stumbling back towards the wall for another push. She was obviously drunk, but she seemed more ill, her eyes half closed as if the sun hurt them, the deep kohl shadows blurring under and around them like bruises, the lopsided crimson gash of her mouth like a shocking wound. Kate had not seen her for a while.

'Jesus,' she said, leaning over the rail. 'She looks half dead.'

'Yeah.' After one heave out of her chair to see over the edge Elsie had not moved.

'She's getting worse, all right. She goes out every night just for enough to buy the booze. I been paying her rent, but she won't eat the food I get her, just lies there holding on to her gin bottle for grim death. I don't think she knows where she is half the time.'

They heard something crash on the stairs. A door opened and there was the sound of shouting and someone's shrill swearing. Elsie drained her glass.

'I better go and see if she's all right,' she said. 'Poor old bugger.'

Kate dressed and stopped at Ivy's room on her way to work. There was no answer to her knock, but she could hear the loud snores from the bed. She called in a couple of times after that, once bringing a half-bottle of gin she had sneaked from the hotel. Although Ivy's tired blue eyes brightened at the sight of the liquor, she seemed too far gone to know who Kate was. In fact, by her feeble movements towards her clothing, she seemed to think it might be a generous customer, waiting for his satisfaction. Kate patted her dry forehead and put the gin on the table near the bed. By now Ivy was coughing all the time, and, apart from swigging at whatever alcohol Elsie and Kate could bring her, doing little but sleeping.

'If she's lucky the cough'll carry her off before she gets the horrors from the drink,' Elsie said grimly. 'It's the consumption if you ask me, from those nights she was too drunk to crawl home in the cold.'

They called the doctor in, Kate and Elsie paying his fee. He told them what they already knew, that it was only a matter of time. They continued to try to get her to take soup or warmed milk, but in her increasingly rare moments of consciousness, with much gasping and choking, she asked only for gin.

'She's going to die anyway,' Elsie said. 'She may as well go drunk.'

They took it in turns to sleep with her, on a pallet made up on the floor. The landlady was impatient for the room, but as long as they paid the rent she could not evict. When Ivy woke they tried to force soft bread soaked in wine into her mouth, but she would not swallow it. She was dying of starvation as much as tuberculosis.

With the broken nights, Kate's days at the hotel became sleep-haunted ordeals that she dragged through, sometimes drowsing on her feet behind the bar if it was not busy. When Scott asked solicitously after her health she snapped at him and saw the hard vengeful squint before he turned away.

One night she got home to find that Ivy was dead.

'She just didn't wake up,' Elsie said with satisfaction, sucking noisily. 'Not a bad way to go, eh? If you've gotta go at all, that is.' She gave her loud laugh, the tears gathering in the wrinkles at the corner of her eyes.

They could not afford to bury her, so they stood shivering in the winter winds on the outskirts of the general paupers' funeral at the end of that week. There was already someone else in Ivy's room – the landlady had reluctantly accepted her meagre furniture in lieu of the last week's rent. There had been no belongings except a tatty fox fur which Elsie kept. They gave the clothes to the rag man for a few pennies.

Kate did not go back to the hotel – her anger at Scott was so great she really feared what she might do if she had to see him again. Elsie defiantly went and got the two days' pay owing. Kate thought of the theatre again but was humiliated at the thought of auditioning.

Elsie took her to see a man who was in charge of booking travelling shows at a tent theatre near the markets, and he promised to remember her. For a breathless moment she thought of telling him who she was, but the memory of Maggie's disapproval still sickened her. She did say that she could do anything on a horse: tricks or bareback riding. The man did not seem very interested, but he wrote it down.

4
The Professor

JONAS ELLMORE SAMPLE – or Professor Sample as the gaudy posters outside the tent proclaimed – was Kate's new boss. As his assistant, her tasks were, at first, laughably easy. She was the plant who sat in the audience and volunteered at the right moment to ride the tamed horses. Or, at other times, she was the owner of a difficult mount, leading it struggling to the round matting-covered dais where the professor carried out his amazing schooling techniques. These horses, loaned from the livery stables across the river, usually calmed down after only a few minutes of his soothing voice and firm, caressing strokes – the removal of the burrs from under their saddles may have had something to contribute as well.

Later, when he trusted her, he let her do some of the actual handling on stage, paying a boy to be the audience volunteer if he needed one, though it was often unnecessary. Anyone would do once the horse was gentled. Kate also helped him with his preparations, which involved elaborate arrangements of fences and barrels, around which the dociled horses would ultimately parade. In small towns they stayed long enough to receive a genuinely wild pony one week and show it, four or five days later, broken and meek, high-stepping round the ring, head reined high, only a slight dullness of eye betraying the copious sedative in its evening mush. Not that it was all sham. Along the way the professor did take some unbroken horses and return them later, on his way back through that district, properly and sedately mounted and trained. Kate had a lot to do with this as she was a first-class breaker.

In town Elsie helped them at the intervals of the shows, but when they travelled Kate had to sway down the straggly aisles with fruit and cakes and the little sugar-covered nuts an old woman in Adelaide made for the professor.

For the shows she wore a tailored, red riding outfit with a tight-waisted jacket and a skirt that flared over leather high-heeled boots. If she sometimes swaggered slightly it was only that she realised how well she looked and accepted the audience's admiration.

Jonas Sample was an educated man – English – who mumbled of older brothers and depleted fortunes. In his tent at night, before they crept beneath the fur-lined rugs on his soft palliasse he read from large leather-bound books, often taking notes in his spidery, hesitant handwriting in a small notebook he carried with him everywhere. He himself was far from hesitant: corpulent and jocular, he spoke always in a loud voice. Even his impatient whispers to the wings during a precarious moment on stage were hissing and sibilant enough to reach the first few rows of those seated on the folding canvas chairs or sprawling on the grassy floor.

High-coloured and deep-voiced, he still had something shifty about him that Kate recognised, from her Irish uncles perhaps, and he was always hurrying to leave a town after a week. Kate liked him, but she never told him who she was, though he tempted her sometimes.

'Ned Kelly!' he said once, startling her into dropping her hairbrush as she prepared for bed. After a frozen moment she looked at him and saw that he was reading from a magazine.

'Some fool here says he should have been sent to war and then his courage would have been give a decent outlet, and not been warped into the monstrous shape it took.' He was not the sort of man who spat, but saliva apparently gathered.

'Oh?' She waited.

'When will they learn?' Kate relaxed, he was delivering one of his favourite lectures. 'Call themselves Christians! Call themselves human beings! They besmirch everything they touch with their mealy-mouthed moral judgements.' Then he did spit. 'I beg your pardon, my dear.' He was always polite with her and treated her like a lady, even in his bed handling her with courtesy, never forgetting to thank her when it was finished.

He stirred her to none of the passion and watchfulness she had known with Joe (whose name she still could not utter, even in thought, the words refusing to form themselves in her mind). But because of his warmth and consideration she might have stayed with him a long time if events had not prevented it, at least until he had taught her everything he knew – a culmination she, ignorantly, thought possible.

He did teach her many things in their months together, some of which, like his love for poetry and portentous sounding prose she would spend years of her life concealing. She always remembered it as a time of calm – enforced calm, she must have known even then, from her frequent and still violent nightmares. If she was indiscreet in these unconscious struggles – that sleeping pain – he never referred to it. Since, although he was polite he was also a man who would not let go of any subject until he had exhausted it – extracted its 'essence' in his words – she assumed she made no shameful revelations. Dimly she may have realised that the day, the reckoning, was only being postponed, but what was still vigorous and healthy in her tried to encyst and forget. There were days, particular times of each month before she menstruated, when this was hard, when headaches and anxiety surfaced like the rising bubbles of some seething mess which any second would overflow and run everywhere, staining her whole life with unthinkable colour. Fortunately, there was always so much to do that she was able to keep on whatever lid of apparent sanity she had, even if it meant sometimes finding herself standing absolutely still, her hands pressed hard to her head as if to stem a real eruption.

Now, perhaps, began her lifelong dependence on the powders and tablets which at least dulled the nerve-endings if they did not cauterise the pain. Now, too, sitting quietly reading by wavering candlelight in their canvas home, she became used to the pleasure of continuously sipping at a glass of alcohol. In those days it was the sipping which comforted.

⊖

Coming into Adelaide after some months away they saw Cole's Circus assembling in paddocks near their own usual stand. They had done well this trip, and the professor reckoned they could afford a holiday. There was no point in setting up in opposition to Cole's anyway. They would go to the circus, enjoy themselves for once, instead of eternally providing other people's enjoyment, he said.

After they had stabled their horses and seen to the wagons, they strolled, arm in arm, along the dusty street to where the Big Tent was being heaved upright. Kate looked with envy at the browned women in breeches rubbing down the circus ponies. Others, who would later wear leotards and spangles, lounged in the open flaps of carts or stood watching as the animals were groomed. Kate had tried to persuade the professor that his act would be improved by some acrobatic bareback riding. Visions of herself in net and tinsel still flickered hopefully. He had not yet agreed, but he had certainly been impressed when, after secret practising, she had ridden three horses abreast, with only leading reins, around and around their campfire one evening, darkly reminiscent to him of some ancient upflung warrior, Boadicea perhaps, against the blazing flamingo dusk.

But as they turned to take their leisurely walk towards the lodging-house where Elsie still lived, and where they hoped to stay for a few days, everything changed. A woman came out from behind a side-show tent and saw them and stopped dead, staring at the professor. She retreated so fast she almost seemed to fall backwards into the canvas, but not before the professor had also seen her. He did not turn pale or gasp but his eyes became thoughtful and fixed, and his grip on Kate's wrist tightened. They walked on, slightly faster than before.

'Who was that? Do you know her?' Kate would not have been surprised by a vengeful wife.

'Oh,' the professor stopped and looked behind them. They had turned a corner and could no longer see the paraphernalia of the circus. He looked down at Kate as if he had forgotten who she was, walking beside him in this provincial street. He seemed to make a secret decision, his gaze became regretful.

'Oh, it is only someone I thought to have been rid of a long time ago. And,' he added almost too quietly for Kate to hear, 'in a very far-off place. Who would have guessed it? Well, who could have guessed?'

'Is she . . .? Could she harm you in some way?' The idea of a wife persisted.

'No. Not she. But she has . . . certain companions. All in all,' he was cheerful, his mind made up, his voice loud and confident again, 'all in all I think it might be best if I don't accompany you to Elsie's place just now. No. But,' he held up a restraining finger, 'but, I shall be in touch. Yes I shall, you can count on that.' They walked on.

At the door he gave her a small wad of paper money and said he would meet her in two days, at the stables. She was not to try to find him before then, when he hoped to have something worked out.

When he did not appear at the appointed time she knew,

even before she asked at the livery stable, that she would not see him again. The horses, the wagons, the comforting cave of his small tent were all gone. That note in his voice had been unmistakable – exactly the tone of sincerity and hearty promise that he used on stage for the least reliable of his demonstrations, precisely the pitch and modulation employed for the greatest lies about his poor bemused horses. Kate had not even bothered to bring her bags.

One night she woke up, feeling herself begin to bleed all over the sheets, too late to try to hold in the slippery hope of the child that this time she had known about from the beginning and had not intended to get rid of. She lay rigid, while the blood oozed for what seemed like hours but could not have been, since by morning she was still alive and did not even feel particularly weak.

She shifted herself cautiously, expecting the sticky gush to begin again, but it did not. She first sponged herself and took off her shift, then without looking at it, bundled up the sheet and its jellied mess, and left it on the ruined mattress, since she didn't know what to do with it. Making her way to Elsie's room she found there was weakness after all, and she was half fainting by the time Elsie came with a large box to remove the bedding. It would take the last of Kate's money to replace the sheets, and the mattress would never be really clean again, although Elsie scrubbed at it with cloths and diluted caustic soda.

'I never thought life would be so terrible,' Kate said weakly, hoping to make Elsie laugh, but she stood up and looked at her seriously.

'Perhaps you should go back to your family,' she said. 'You've a married sister haven't you?' She did not mention whatever other relatives she must guess at. 'I reckon your cough's got worse, too. You don't want to end up like poor old Ivy.'

'It's only a chest cold, from the nights in the tent.' But she thought it was the fits of hacking coughs that had brought on the miscarriage.

Later, lying on her freshly covered bed, she wondered if it was time to go back, but the thought of spending the rest of her life in the obscure drudgery of the farmyard terrified her. She would leave it a while, until the weather improved. You never knew what might be around the corner, waiting.

5
Greta

AGAIN THE TWO women sat in a railway carriage facing each other. They both looked older and worn. They had just left the hospital at Beechworth where Maggie had come to fetch Kate home. For two months the doctors would not hold out any hope of recovery – she was too far gone, they said, she should have sought treatment earlier.

She had gone to a doctor in Adelaide who gave her foul-tasting placebos and refused to diagnose her condition as serious. Elsie, her hard fat face resigned, had given her the fare to Melbourne. Kate did not know that it was Elsie, too, who caused the message to be sent to her family in Greta, so that they were at least partly prepared for the thin, half-dead girl who at last dragged herself through the gate at Spencer Street Station and burst into tears and coughing when she saw them there. She had never asked how they knew to meet her; perhaps in her near delirious state she imagined she had written to them herself.

They had taken her straight home to the Eleven Mile Creek, but after a day they saw she would have to go to the hospital. No one thought she would live.

'Home,' she said, looking out of the window, with a small high gasp and a sigh. It was early winter, the bush grey and dormant, shadows of chilly mist creeping upwards into the dull twilight, the gums, silver or blue in the summer, now a uniform leathery black against the grey sky.

Maggie heard the wheeze in her voice and was alarmed. She leaned forward and pulled Kate's shawl tighter around her thin shoulders.

'Are you warmly dressed enough? I should have brought the rug.'

Kate shrugged, but kindly. Maggie thought, she has softened. There was a sadness, almost resignation in her smile.

'I'll be all right. There's no need to fuss.'

Jim was waiting at the station with the cart, and he had thought to bring a blanket, which they both wrapped around her, over her head and shoulders and tucked into Jim's coat which he put over her knees. They forgave her everything she had done or not done – she had come home.

❧

Again she convalesced, but more actively, gently trotting her mother's mare around the dirt roads which now criss-crossed the district from the new selections to the town and the railroad. She avoided Bricky's property. Although the Kellys never really believed he betrayed Ned's whereabouts to have his sentence shortened, still a sort of distaste hung about the thought of him. Perhaps they thought they deserved to be betrayed, having brought him so much trouble. The family told her that he lived an even more solitary life than before, working his meagre land, keeping to himself in his half-built shack, a dog or two for company. Sometimes Jim rode over to visit him, and they walked about the property inspecting fences or kicking at rabbit holes, but otherwise the family had nothing to do with him any more.

So Kate rode the long way round, past the river banks and over the wooden bridge, sometimes ending up at Maggie's, almost accidentally.

Now that Bill was home they had begun to make their place more like a farm. They had horses and pigs and a growing flock of chickens which squawked and flapped out of the way when Kate rode into the yard. There was order in their place and the promise of comfort and growth. Bill never talked about his time in prison. He and Maggie were always working, they had most of their land cleared and were putting in their first crops this year. Already they had a small field of lush lucerne and a large, well-weeded kitchen garden, finely raked and composted, waiting to deliver rows of fresh beans and cabbages.

The air seemed calmer here, Kate thought, the straggly bush further away, as if Maggie could soothe the earth itself to her own peaceful patterns. She had two children now and a baby. Kate liked to sit in a bamboo chair under the unfinished verandah with the infant on her knees, watching Maggie at work in the garden. The baby smelled clean, and mewed and bubbled softly against her chest, which still moved in and out too shallowly and too fast. It was a girl, named Kathleen for her.

The oldest boy, who had spent his babyhood without his father, often came to stand beside her when he finished his own chores, and she told him about the circuses she had watched and the tricks she could do on a pony herself. His parents told him she was not strong, so he did not ask to see these tricks, but his fingers twitched. He would have liked to swoop from the backs of galloping horses like the man he saw once in a travelling show, and he found it hard to believe that his slow-moving frail little aunt might have dared, too.

Kate's own aunt and other namesake, Kate Lloyd, came down the river sometimes to visit at the Kellys. She had become thin-faced and shrill, although she and Jack had prospered and now had men working for them on their property, paid real wages. But by now everyone believed it was the Lloyds that had dobbed in the bushranger Harry Power – when he was hiding out at the Quinn's place at Glenmore – and pocketed the reward, and Jack never accompanied his wife and children on these family visits, pretending he had risen above such as the Kellys and the Quinns. Not that anyone ever said anything to his face – the sour words were whispered round like gossip but the welcoming smiles would still have greeted him at the door.

Kate Lloyd was always urging Kate to leave again, as soon as she was well.

'You got away once,' she said. 'Don't be foolish enough to get caught here now.'

'I don't know.' For the time being Kate was relieved to have no rent to pay and her meals provided twice a day. She had not allowed herself to think about what would happen after she was well again. She knew her mother and Jim hoped she would stay, although they hadn't said anything. Jim was old before his time, she thought, yet their mother hadn't changed very much – they could almost be a man with his old wife running the farm together and bringing up Gracie and the younger children. It was all comforting, certainly, and nothing new would be allowed to happen here, where so much had already happened. She acknowledged that she would probably leave again.

'Why don't you go to Albury or somewhere? It's not so far away, and there'd be plenty of work there, surely. When you're strong enough of course.' Kate Lloyd knew someone who lived there, a sister-in-law.

'Maybe. I'll have to wait until the summer whatever happens. The doctor says I mustn't think of working again before then.'

But she knew she could not remain where she had ridden

102

with Joe Byrne and her brothers almost everywhere. Even the new raw roads carried their hovering ghosts, dangerous triggers to God knew what destructive memories. She would never allow that reason to come to the surface of her thoughts, but she had already decided not to stay.

PART THREE

1

WHEN I WALK ALONG the lagoon here and look back past the willows to the town it reminds me of the years I spent in Albury, after I was recovering from the consumption. There is something very similar in all large country towns, I think. Albury at first reminded me of Adelaide, with its wide streets and the rows of peppercorns, frilly as jacarandas, though Mrs Ponter's Promenade Hotel, where I worked, was not at all like Bill Scott's South Adelaide Hotel.

Mrs Ponter was an Englishwoman with pale hair and a closed, hard face. A lady, she said she had been, before her husband fell on hard times. I could see she was a lady all right, in the same way that Jonas Sample was a gentleman, with a lot left out and best untold. She and I did not like each other, but we did not have to. There was no reason as far as she was concerned to associate with me at all unless I failed to please.

My room there was in the attic with the other live-in servants, and it too reminded me of my little room in the boarding-house and Elsie, who I will never see again in this life, although I often wonder how she is. There was a table under the window, with a pink washbasin and jug and a bar of cracked yellow soap in a dish.

Every morning I would stand there in the golden light that came through the low window, rubbing the cold facecloth over my face and shoulders; looking out over the shops and houses and paddocks, right across the river to the flats and scrubby foothills where my brothers often rode across the border with Joe Byrne; watching the first sun lightening the valleys, straining for what I knew I would never see – the growing shapes of four men on their horses.

It was serving at the bar that I met Ben Roberts. He had to come to Albury sometimes on business, and he took to coming in the evenings when he knew I would be there.

'It gets lonely for a bloke like me,' he said one night, having drunk more than usual. 'It's the missus – She's never been strong, and these days she's practically bedridden. It makes it hard.' He looked at me quickly, then gazed into his beer.

I knew what he meant. I was lonely too, with my changed name, not daring to look up any of our relatives or old friends in the town. I knew what he meant when he said he needed some comfort and affection.

That night I met him after work and we walked slowly through the sleeping streets, talking about horses and farming and the cattle station he managed out in the middle of New South Wales. We went back to his room in another hotel, it seemed natural to do so. The servants' door at Mrs Ponter's was left unlocked, a thing she never knew, so I would have no trouble getting in later.

After that, on my days off, whenever Ben was in town we would go in his cart to the nearby shows, where he would let me help inspect the horses he was buying. Or we would admire the bulls that came from his own place, often with a prize ribbon around their necks. When we had finished the serious business we would stroll through the sideshows and tents, stopping to watch the bare-knuckle boys challenging the louts in the crowd, or to gaze at the posters of bearded ladies or two-headed men. Sometimes we went inside those tents, but anyone could see they were not real freaks, not like the dwarves and the poor hermaphrodite we saw one day. We bought sherbets and sat and watched the show-jumping, and I would itch to ride out there in the ring, as Maggie and I and the boys used to do when we were young.

At night we went back to his room. This was nothing like the feeling I had for Joe – that impetuousness of young animals full of impatience, when we fell into each other's arms under bushes, against trees, or breathlessly close to my sleeping brothers in the mountain camps. But it was comforting, at a time when I needed comfort, and Ben did much to help me heal the terrible griefs I still bore.

Sometimes he would sit on the bed where I lay, naked, tracing the outlines and shadows of my body with his fingertips, gently, urgently, as if he could absorb something of me through the pores of his own skin. It would put me to sleep, and then I would wake to find his body already joined to mine, my own limbs thrusting at him from out of a dream. It was not love; I did not think it. I thought I had had my one bitter taste of that and it would not happen again.

⌢

We were walking one evening in late winter along the grassy banks of the river. We had been at a horse show where I gazed for a long time at a tall black mare. I had on a new dress of soft light wool and a velvet jacket from the days when my brothers threw their money about, and I felt well, healthy for the first time in nearly a year and as contented as I could remember being. Ben looked sideways at me as we walked along, and I was pleased at thinking that I looked my best.

'You liked that mare then?'

'Yes. She was lovely. It is a pity your boss won't breed them

– she would be fine brood stock.' I was talking idly, and what he said next gave me a shock.

'Would you like to have her?'

I stopped and looked at him. His red face was worried, he was holding his breath for my answer. Back along the river there were early picnickers sitting on their pale cloths in the deep green grass. I laughed.

'Of course I would. But where would I keep a horse at the pub?'

We walked on, and I tucked my hand hard under his arm, thinking how I would look racing along the river banks on that fine dark horse. Ben was silent too, and I began to think he was serious. When we came to a seat near the bridge he pulled me down and we sat looking out across the brown water. I waited to hear what he would say next.

'You've heard me talk of Cadow Station, that's only a dozen miles from us?'

'Yes. Why?'

'They're wanting a domestic.' He took a deep breath and plunged on. 'Someone to help in the kitchen during the mustering, and a bit of general housekeeping.' He looked down at his hat that he was twisting between his knees. 'Well. I thought – you could have a horse then, like you always say you want.'

Now he waited for me to speak. I was happy enough at the Promenade, but the hope of a horse set me dreaming, and the thought of a new place, far away from the danger of people coming grinning to the door asking for Kate Kelly that works in the hotel.

'I don't know. I will have to think about it.' Already I could think of nothing else.

We walked back in the cold breeze of the sudden dusk, and when he left me at the hotel he gave me a piece of paper with the name of the manager at Cadow on it.

'Let me know if you decide . . . I can easily put in a good

word for you there.'

We said goodbye, and as he turned away he muttered something else.

'What?' I said. 'What was that you said?'

'I said, I'll get you that mare if you do.' He walked off, and I stood staring at him until he crossed the street and rounded the corner out of sight.

❧

I was at Cadow two years when Ben was sent north to manage another station owned by his boss, Mr McDougall. He wanted me to go with him, he was sure he could find me a place there, but we had quarrelled a lot that last year, and to tell the truth I was not unhappy at his going. He was very angry with me when I became friends with Ethel, the cook, and would sometimes have a few drinks with her of an evening.

'You have to be careful,' he said to me. 'If you get a bad name it will reflect on me, as I recommended you.'

And, I thought, because everyone knew of his visits to me at Cadow and he worried about *his* good name and his wife finding out. He had changed after I came to the station and perhaps regretted persuading me when he realised I would not spend my time only waiting for his visits but wanted some life of my own as well. But when he left he let me keep the mare, Shadow, which was generous of him, and I think of him now with fondness for the good times.

I liked the life of the station, and being out in the open again, with the horses, but after Ben went I was restless, and when Ethel's friend Janet Frost said that Mrs Prow in Forbes was wanting a servant I was eager to go. I still thought I had not had my fill of gaiety and bustle, and I hankered after the amusements of a town again. Now I often wish I had stayed, with only the horses and the housework and the countryside to answer to, growing old alone in the bush, as I feel I was meant to do.

2

I WAS MARRIED in the summer at the Church of England in Brandon Street. I wore a lacy dress that Maude and Ethel, my sisters-in-law, helped me make, and carried lilies of the valley bought from Mr Luthie, the undertaker. My mother could not travel all this way – she was not well – and Maggie was in childbed, but Jim came to stand beside me in the church.

I cried with happiness to see him, my quiet brother, elderly before his time, and I asked him to stay for a while after the wedding. And he did, making shoes for us all – a trade he had got very good at. He stayed in Forbes until I was sure I was expecting Freddie, and when he left he said he would make some special boots of white calfskin in time for the baby to take its first steps . . .

❧

'I would like to call our first child Edward,' I said to Bill. We were sitting together in the drawing-room of his family's house. They lived in the main street of Forbes then, in a wide brick house that reminded me of my grandfather's place at Glenmore, although it was finer than any house my family ever lived in. But there was the same coming and going of all the family through the cool shaded rooms, the same feeling that here was the hub of many people's lives, the starting point of family gossip and feuds.

He took his hand from my neck and turned away from me. I had not expected the room would get so quiet, waiting for his reply.

'I don't think that would be a good idea. I hoped we might call it for my grandfather, if it is a boy.'

'I thought you did not care about – what is past,' I said. I had told him everything, when we were courting: walking in the hot spring sun along the lagoon, on picnics with his sisters, in the buggy going to the show. Everything, except what I could never tell anyone, about Joe Byrne. He had said it did not matter; that he admired Ned Kelly and all he stood for; that he was proud to know his sister. But they are a respectable family, the Farmers: my brothers-in-law are on the town council and are members of all the busy committees of the place.

'I don't. But what's done is done. It does no good to rake it up again.' He turned back to me and kissed me softly on the mouth. I gave in. He was kind and handsome then, and my heart beat faster when I saw him, though I cannot credit it now. It is almost impossible to bring back the memory of what we were like – really like – in those days.

⌒

I was twenty-six when we met, and had made up my mind, I suppose, that I would not marry, with Ivy's fate always staring me in the eye. Bill was twenty-three. It was while I was working at Prow's as a domestic. Sometimes Mrs Prow asked me to go down to the shop with a message for her husband, or to fetch something she needed for the house.

I suppose I had seen him before, as he came often into Prow's shop, buying gear for his horses, but this day I heard his name, or the name his mates called him, and it startled me into really looking. I was standing near the counter, waiting to see Mr Prow, when I caught the phrase, 'Ah, go on Bricky, you wouldn't . . .' and then some laughter. He told me later that he was trying to get up the courage to talk to me. Certainly, when I swung around he was staring in my direction, and must have been surprised at my look of shock and then relief. Of course I knew it could not be *our* Bricky, there, in Forbes, hundreds of miles from home, but it startled me.

I thought of him sometimes after that day, the way he stared at me and the dull blush when I caught him at it, and I made excuses to go to the shop more often in case he was there. But when we met again it was by accident.

It was in summer (it seems always summer in my memory, while now is cold and bare), and in his open shirt and stockman's rough trousers he reminded me I suppose, of Ned and Dan and Joe, and the days gone forever. And – although it is unbelievable now – he did, then, at first, remind me of Joe in other ways. The same springy hair and grey Irish eyes; that saucy, confident look to him, used to getting his own way, you could see. With all this I made myself interested, against my better judgement perhaps, as we sometimes will.

I had gone to a cattle show with Janet Frost and Ethel, the cook from Cadow Station, and we had hired a dray. The day was cloudy and threatened with rain so we huddled under the canvas outside the pavilion to watch the judging of the woodchop and then the trick riding. Ethel nudged me and said, perhaps too loudly, 'Go on Ada, love. You should be out there in that ring. Better rider than all them blokes put together.'

We had had a few swigs from Ethel's gin on the way. I looked round to see if anyone noticed and saw the man they called Bricky staring at me again.

Perhaps I was reckless, having sipped the bottle, or perhaps

114

I had decided already, but I gave him a wave and a small smile to see what he would do. He got up slowly and came over to us. I pretended not to notice him until he spoke.

'Bill Farmer,' he said. 'I seen you at Prow's the other day.'

Ethel and Janet looked at me, then half turned their backs, smiling. They were too old themselves to be on the lookout, and Ethel always said she preferred the bottle any day, to put her to sleep.

I think I was let down from the very first, but would not allow myself to know it. He had a rough voice, unschooled, and I pushed away the thought that his mouth looked weak – I had already let myself have ideas about him, and it was almost too late to turn back.

'Ada,' I said. 'Ada Hennessey. But my friends call me Kate.'

'I know. I asked about you at Prow's.' He looked at Ethel and Janet but they kept themselves turned away. 'Like to look at the sideshows or something?'

'All right,' I said, and to the others, 'I'll meet you at the cart later.' Ethel gave me a knowing smile.

We walked round the tents a while, and when it started to rain properly we went inside the pavilion to look at the domestic exhibits. He pointed out proudly the cakes and embroidery his sisters and mother had on display, with their gold and blue rosettes.

Later we went deeper under the canvas for tea and cakes, and sat at folding tables eating, not talking much – he has never been much of a talker, and I was still turning over in my mind whether I would want him or not. But I did not go home with Ethel and Janet, and from then on we were courting.

I know there was the excitement and the impatience of all courting couples, but now I cannot revive those feelings at all – it is as if they happened to another person. Yet in my mind I see quite clearly, like a sequence of pictures on a diorama, the woman that was me, going off after work at night, brushing her long black hair, pinching her cheeks to make them pink, flashing dark eyes at the mirror and running, running, down the stairs, out the door, along the street. We went to dances, all the shows at the Victoria, and the Wax Works where a harpist played Irish ballads and where I feared to find effigies of my brothers, and was half disappointed not to find them. And on warm nights we walked along the lagoon, under willows, too caught up in ourselves to see the dog carcasses and human shit washing around the shoreline. (Now I walk around the lagoon alone, and see everything.)

I catch myself looking at Bill these days, when he is at home, which is not all that often, trying to find that slicked-down young man with the new boots polished almost transparent who waited, endlessly, leaning against the lamp-post in the street outside the house, pacing in front of the dance hall, or on Sundays sitting, hat in hand, in Mrs Prow's second-best parlour before taking me to church. That young, eager man whose face flushed red, then deathly pale whenever he saw me, whose love shone in his eyes strongly enough, I thought, to keep me safe forever.

❧

After Freddie was born we took over the livery stables in Rankin Street, and some of that time is still clear in my mind. How I loved that familiar smell of the horses, even our clothing was saturated with it. It was a brief space of great contentment to me, working, riding, grooming, feeding, the baby in his basket beside me, or later toddling around underfoot, him knowing the rhythms of a horse before he could walk on his own feet, as we all did. But of course, as my mother always said, the good times do not last and it is only foolishness to think they will.

❧

Bill came in one day where I was working in the kitchen and

I could see he was angry. He threw his hat on the table and stood glaring at me. He was always slow to begin an argument because he knew I would outwit him more times than not, although it sometimes cost me a black eye or a cut lip. He was fast with his hand, however slow he was to speak.

'You've been showing off down the park again,' he said. 'Daniel Jones said he seen you there this afternoon. Riding round in circles, he said, hollering and doing tricks, drawing the crowd.'

I knew he would find out, but had hoped it would not be so soon. I wiped my sweating hands on the apron.

'Well, the colts have to be broken by someone.' I tried to keep my voice quiet and steady. I was pregnant again, with Gertie, and I felt her jerking inside me like my own heartbeat. 'They need the exercise. The colts must be schooled before they get too old.'

'You know what I'm talking about. There's a difference between breaking them in like anyone would, and skiting about, behaving like a hoyden. Standing up on horses' backs, taking dares to ride three at once, Daniel said, and God knows what else you done after he left.' His face was red and twisted up from such a long speech, and he was breathing hard in anger. 'Have you forgotten that you're expecting a child?'

I knew what would come next, I waited, my lips drawn tight together.

'Have you forgotten what happened last time?'

He could always defeat me with this argument. He knew I could not stay composed at the thought of that perfect child born dead after so much pain and blood. I had planned to call him Joseph.

'It was not riding that killed him. The cord was twisted. I rode before Freddie was born without it hurting him.' But I was muttering. I knew I could not go on with this.

'Well, I am going to put a stop to it once and for all. There is a bloke interested in buying what's left of our lease.'

'No!' I could not believe he would be so vindictive. 'No. Please. Billy, don't take the horses away from me. I will not do any more breaking until after the child is born, I promise.'

'Or drinking either?' His big man's sneer. I sat down, knowing I was lost. I did not think he knew about that; I was trying to keep it hidden.

He went to the dresser and took down the unmarked bottle. He pulled the cork and poured the gin down the sink.

'There'll be no more of that,' he said, and looked at me defiantly. At least he did not know about the laudanum that I was still getting from Vanzetti's, the chemists. I kept that under a loose board in the wash-house.

'It was just a sip now and then,' I said softly. 'I still have the back pains as you know.' It was true, and the pregnancy was making it worse.

(Now that I am pregnant once more I am afraid of the winter drawing close and that deep terrible ache beginning again when the baby gains some weight inside me. Sometimes it feels as though there is something torn or broken deep inside me from that infant that was born dead, an injury that will never heal.)

'All the more reason not to go near the horses.'

That was when I began to hate him, I think, his triumphant, mean smile, his easy victory. But what could I do? A woman expecting a child with a small boy already dragging round me, and weak from three pregnancies in a row? I might have gone home to my family at Greta, but the life there would be no improvement – the chores of the farm and the neighbours who already knew too much about me.

He was surprised, though, at the depth of my despair when he did sell the lease. He came home with the money and I ranted and shouted and tried to hit him. He did not slap me back, but held me, not unkindly, until I was through. But he would not change his mind. He was going to keep a couple of the horses and find work for himself around the town, he

118

said, there being many people needing someone who had his expertise. I think he was tired of all the work of the stables and welcomed the excuse to get rid of them, but to me it was the taking away of my main pleasure in life. I still kept my mare, Shadow, but I had loved the feel and the smell of the stables, forking into the solid bales of hay, the chaff dribbling through my fingers as a horse snuffled in my palm with its soft lips.

✎

After Gertie was born they told me my condition was common to many women after childbirth and that I would recover in time and take up my life again, as I had after Fred's birth. But I knew it was deeper than that; it was not only the weakness from the loss of blood and the body's struggle to regain its balance. And in the end they knew it too, though I remember little of the details of those lost months. They promise me it should not happen after this next child, but they do not realise that it has never stopped, that it was deep in me always, that I look at Gertie playing on the floor now, her thin arms and nervous eyes, and my flesh crawls at the thought of an infant once more suckling blind-eyed at my sore breasts, the soiled swaddling lying in smelly heaps, the bleeding and the messiness of it all . . .

✎

They had handed her the baby girl wrapped tight in flannel, and she turned her pale face to the wall, her arms lying limp along the coverlet. She could hear the doctor and the midwife whispering urgently, and she felt the doctor's hand on her forehead.

'She has a slight fever perhaps,' he said to the old woman putting the baby back into its cradle. 'Leave the child for now and try her with it again in the morning.'

119

The old woman sat by the bed all night, occasionally tiptoeing heavily across to look anxiously at the sleeping baby. She had delivered more babies than she could remember, and she knew the signs. The baby girl was pale and thin, as if it were she and not the mother who was the drunk and the opium addict. The midwife was surprised that the woman did not ask for one or the other during the long night, but Kate, feverish and half asleep, was having her own dreams easily enough . . .

The room swirled around her, figures wafted close and away, stood talking just out of earshot, almost out of vision. Sometimes she strained from the bed towards them, but her limbs were too heavy to lift. In her pain and confusion she was dreaming, or wishing, her brothers and Joe Byrne alive. In the distance came the call of a train's whistle, like the ship's horn, she thought, on the day that she and Maggie, swashbuckling in their sweeping fashionable skirts and feathered hats strode elegantly along the pier at Port Melbourne.

They had swayed up the gangplank watched by the admiring sailors, and they smiled at each other secretly when the captain appeared, a young man, clearly charmed and flustered by their presence on his ship.

Maggie had allowed her dimples to show at his youthful blush.

'We wish to book passage for some gentlemen – relatives,' Maggie said, while Kate twirled her gloves and pointed her feet to admire her new boots, allowing the captain's appreciative glance to take them in also before she arranged the folds of her dress more demurely to cover her ankles.

'How many gentlemen would that be?' He was polite. They thought the excitement in his eyes was for their presence alone – they did not know that all ships' captains had been asked to watch for exactly such an occurrence, that the minute they left he would send his messengers to the police, that in his mind's eye he already saw himself collecting the citation from the Governor of Victoria.

'Oh, four or five, we are not sure yet,' said Kate. 'We only came to find out if there are berths available.'

'Of course,' the captain said. 'I'll show you what we have.' He took them to the little cabins himself and then showed them the rest of the ship, seating them on deck chairs while a white-coated steward fetched lemon ices and biscuits.

They made lively conversation, enlarging their story about their cousins who wished to try their luck prospecting in California. They thought they had him twisted around their little fingers. They thought they had got away with it, had got away with everything after all.

∽

Now, Kate, in her febrile post-partum drowsiness, twists and squirms away from the pictures *that* terrible mistake conjures up.

∽

Walking briskly back along the docks, almost running in their glee that they had got away with it, Maggie and Kate made their own plans. They would join the men later, Jim and their mother too, if they could. They'd go prospecting, all of them. Perhaps Kate and Maggie would ride in a Wild West Act – they could show the Americans some things about horse riding. They'd get rich and buy a ranch and spend their days breeding cattle and horses and thumbing their noses at the Victorian Police. They hurried back to the hotel where Ned and Dan and Joe waited, with Steve and Wild Wright, bursting with laughter and confidence.

Fantasies swirl now in Kate's mind, of herself, dressed in black lace, a purple satin bodice, leaning over Joe's shoulder

121

as he plays cards in some Californian hotel, like a scene in a three-act play they saw once, put on by travelling players.

❧

She calls out his name, waking the midwife, but not the baby in its prenatally drugged sleep, and as she moans 'Joe, Joe,' that other picture, the one always subconsciously associated with his name, struggles its way into her dreaming vision, causing perspiration to break out all over her body, and her limbs to thrash out of the bedsheets. And she sits upright, wide awake now, staring, shouting 'No! No!' while his propped body, charred, bloated, smarmed with the sheepish smile of death, sways and slips down the wall of her memory.

❧

They brought the baby to her again in the morning and every hour or so during the day, but she would not hold it, and they had to stand close to the bed, for she would really let it roll off, it seemed.

'If we could only get it to suck,' the midwife muttered to the doctor when he made his visit. 'But I put it to her and she won't close her arms around it, lets it lie as it may, she doesn't seem to care.'

Finally the old woman sat close to the bed, pressing the baby to Kate's breasts as she slept. But it was languid and would not drink heartily. Kate woke, or half woke and let her gaze slide down to the infant's head buried in her bosom, breathed in the sickly smell of blood and milk, and closed her eyes again and slept. She kept her eyes shut when Bill made his visits and stood helplessly by the bed watching the midwife's efforts, but she heard the woman trying to reassure him, and his doubtful reply before he left. They could not afford the old woman for longer than the customary first few days, and in the end Kate's neighbour, Clara, said she would come in four or five times a day and hold the baby to her to feed, which it would do now, though listlessly.

Sometimes Kate woke during that week and seemed surprised to see Clara there, but usually she lay unmoving and let them do what they liked with her, not resisting when she was helped to the washbasin or the chamber-pot, allowing herself to be put in the rocking-chair while Clara and Bill's sisters changed the sheets (she still bled, slightly but continuously), then limply arranging herself again on her pillows when they helped her into bed.

Against all predictions the child began to thrive, and one night Kate was woken by its hungry cry coming from the cradle. Gradually the whimpering grew to an angry bellow, and Kate got slowly out of bed and picked it up. She stood by the cradle staring into the tiny contorted face. She did not smile or cuddle, but she took it back to bed and unlaced her nightgown, holding the baby firmly to her tender nipples as the midwife and Clara had done. When it was finished she left the infant sleeping in the bed beside her, and lay with her gown unbuttoned, staring into the approaching grey shadows of the dawn.

When Bill saw that Kate had finally taken to the baby, he felt able to begin his new job, travelling from town to town with his cart full of gear, working as a farrier for those who did not have their own equipment.

Kate's days were spent more comfortably with him away. She ambled about the dark little house, the toddling boy whining gently around her heels as she did the desultory housework and tended to the placid baby.

'She's too quiet,' Clara told her one day, leaning over the crib with a worried frown. 'She sleeps too much for such a little one. They're the ones usually that cry the most and want to be fed every hour.'

Kate did not seem to hear. She was too quiet herself, dreamy, wafting through the untidiness and dirt of her kitchen with a small smile always on her lips.

'You're not back on the grog, are you?' Clara stared into her friend's face. 'You promised Bill, you know. He'll take the kiddies off you if he thinks you're drinking again.'

'No,' Kate said. 'What makes you say that? My back aches and I take the medicine a bit, that's all. It does make feel a bit sleepy.'

Clara was not reassured, but she went away.

But really Kate was only half awake most of the time. The combination of the gin and the Pink Pills she took three or four times a day kept her barely conscious enough to scrape together the clothes and food needed for daily life with the children.

Much of the day she sat in her bedroom with the blinds still drawn, her hand on the side of the baby's crib, while the little boy, often wet and dirty, played anxiously in the parlour. His monologues, half formed speech and half infant babble, comforted Kate in her constant doze – the intense high chattering voice rising and falling in volume and rhythm like the running of shallow water over small stones seemed in tune somehow with the turgid but unceasing ruminations of her own brain.

She sat, day after day, in her rocking-chair, dreaming herself back in the bush camp with her brothers and Joe Byrne. So deeply were these fantasies ingrained on her mind that if the baby woke, startling her with its weak cry, she would literally pull up short in her chair, her body jerking to a stop, her dulled stare hardly noticing that there were no reins across her lap, that furniture surrounded her, shrouded and claustrophobic, and there was no breeze.

She would take the baby up in her arms, still confused, her soothing mutters somehow connected with the banks of the river and the men squatting round the campfire, so that it seemed Joe's child she held, though without knowing how or why she had come by it.

'Look at her,' she would murmur then. 'Look Joe, Dan. Isn't she pretty? We will put her by the fire for a while, in the sunshine, there.' And she would look around, bewildered, in the dust and dark of the small room, for something that would do as a log or a hummock of grass. Later she would be surprised to find the baby not in her cot, and would search vaguely for her, not understanding how she came to be sleeping across a pile of washing or wedged between the back and seat of the rocking-chair.

When Bill came back – he had written to her but she had not read the letter – his first feeling was of terror that someone had snatched the baby, or that she had died without anyone letting him know. The tearful, grimy small boy and the state of the house did not at first register on his slow mind, only that the baby was missing and then that Kate seemed in the grip of a terrible despair, slatternly and wide-eyed.

Kate looked in the crib.

'Oh,' she said, halting, trying to remember. 'Sometimes she sleeps in strange places . . .' she gestured around the room, and Bill saw now the mess and clutter their house had become. Clothes and newspapers covered the floor and the half of the bed Kate did not use. Dust piled and swayed in the corners. Someone had drawn in what looked like human shit on the mirror of the old wardrobe, and scraps of food lay in the cracks between the floorboards.

By the wall a heap of clothing had been hollowed out and in this soft nest the baby lay, naked, pale and sleeping.

'There's no point in swaddling her,' Kate said, explaining, in a thick slow voice. 'She only wets herself again, and besides the sunlight is good for the skin.' She sat down in the chair and rocked gently, waiting for Bill to agree.

He picked up the baby and left Kate there, rocking and smiling. He took the little boy carefully by the hand and went next door to Clara's, and, trembling with an emotion he could not name, asked her to fix them up and feed them for a couple of days. Clara took them in gratefully – she had been afraid to interfere, she said, and Kate would not open the door, no matter how hard she knocked.

Then he went home and searched every cupboard, throwing away the gin and the syrupy medicine, keeping only the Pink Pills which he still believed she needed for her backaches.

The last gin bottle he emptied in front of her eyes, out of the bedroom window, shaking the drops carefully on the sill.

'You promised me,' he said, 'that you would not touch it while I was away. Now I'm going to see you keep that promise while I am here.'

❧

It took nearly two days for Kate to emerge from her stupor, while Bill sat grimly in the chair beside her bed, refusing her anything but soup and one or two of the Pink Pills when she cried out that her back was killing her.

It began with shaking. As she sat up in bed, her body began to shudder from the thighs to the shoulders, as if the trunk did not belong to the tightly clenched limbs, as if her rigid arms and legs were brittle splints to hold the body's trembling. Then her teeth began to chatter, uncontrollably. She could not force her mouth open over her locked and spasming jaws, and her wild eyes skittered in her head. He had to bend close, his head against her mouth to understand her frantic pleas for a drink. Finally he was frightened and fetched the doctor, who allowed laudanum, in small but frequent doses until the fits had passed.

'She should really be in the hospital,' he said, but Kate's shuddering became so violent at the word and her eyes so desperate that they agreed to see if they could manage her at home.

In the evening of the third day, from being propped shivering in bed, Kate sprang like a tiger cat at Bill when he brought her soup and medicine. Somehow she had crept out and got a kitchen knife to hide under her pillow, and she hurled it with such force that it splintered the door where it struck and stayed, quivering !ike a thrown spear. It would certainly have killed him if her aim had been true, and in the grim silent struggle that followed, if he had not been such a solid-muscled man, she would have severely hurt him, scratching and biting and gouging as if she fought for her life, or her children's.

'Like a bloody maniac,' he said later, not without pride, and with some accuracy, for the unaccustomed adrenalin coursing through her system with the sudden withdrawal of her drugs had produced an effect very like medically induced mania.

She lay sobbing on the bed, without tears, while they tied her into the straitjacket, her limbs still jerking convulsively but no longer intending violence, able to force out one word only, 'Don't! ... Don't!' But they heaved her between two white-coated men and carried her out to the waiting hospital carriage.

3

WHEN I CAME OUT of the hospital we moved in with Bill's family, and things were better again for a while. Mrs Farmer and the girls took care to say nothing of what had happened, and Ethel waited on me like an invalid for some weeks. I could not even then remember much – I knew I had become violent, and I remembered the hospital, where they would not give me anything although I had the shakes and could barely breathe for wanting a drink or a sip of the sweet pink medicine. It seemed like a dream afterwards, all of it, and the baby, Gertie, seemed to have arrived without me noticing how, already cutting her first teeth and sucking on bacon rinds and husks when I first became properly aware of her.

Bill could not stay at home – there were no jobs for him – and anyway he enjoyed the life travelling with his cart, and his physics for the horses. Perhaps I should have gone with him, like a gypsy's wife, bedding the children down under the stars, never having to care about the trouble of getting through the day. But I was too weak and listless and sank gratefully into the rhythms of the Farmers' lives in the big old comfortable house, letting them take control of my life for me.

They had only let me out of the hospital on Bill's promise that I would not be left alone, but he would not give that promise until I had sworn I would stay off the drink and the laudanum.

'I will not have you in my mother's house in the state you were in before,' he said, and I felt he hated me then, his eyes seemed to glitter with contempt, although it may have been pity. I would have promised anything to get out of that place, and I did. The promises were easy enough to keep for a time, frightened as I was of the talk of asylums and my children going into care, and Ethel and Maude took the place of my sister Maggie in my life, soothing and caring for me and not ever referring unkindly to my past behaviour.

It was like being a girl again – there was always Mrs Farmer to take care of the children if I wanted to slip out and see Janet Frost or Clara for the afternoon, but I did not visit them often, for the temptation of the gin bottle always gleamed at me from their kitchen cupboards.

Sometimes I took the children out myself, and it was almost as if I was their sister or their aunt, knowing I could take them back to their grandmother whenever I liked. It was a good, quiet time for all of us. We went on picnics along the river, or to watch the boats on the lagoon, or I took them along to the stables and gave them rides on Shadow. I did not ride myself – I did not seem to have the heart for it – so they used the mare in the livery stables in return for her keep. I have sold her now. I could not bear any longer the reproachful looks she gave when I walked past without stopping to saddle her up, leaving her to be exercised by their paid grooms.

Most of the time I spent by myself, walking by the lagoon, as Bill and I had in the old days, watching the ducks, and the Chinese in their little boats, fishing.

There was a place on the old bridge – perhaps it is still there, I have not been down for a long time – where you could sit on a beam and dangle your legs through a hole rotted in the railings. I have always had a fear of heights, and fainted once when my brothers put me on the roof of their hut in the Wombat Ranges to keep lookout for them. Dan found me unconscious, half fallen over the rooftree, and for a moment, he said, he thought I had been shot. But at first sitting on the bridge, high above the swirling water, was pleasant, safe, the water somehow not as frightening as the thought of hard ground or rocks to fall on. Gradually I noticed it had a pull of its own, too, the brown eddying ripples so soothing and repetitive, washing gently around the slimy uprights of the bridge.

One day I must have sat too close, or too precariously, and almost fell. I was in that trance that moving water can induce, with its pull towards the drowning tide, and only a girl passing with her lover kept me from plunging into its oily coldness. She called out sharply – I had begun to slip – and her young man rushed over and grabbed my arm as I faltered on the edge. The backs of my legs were splintered from the rough planks.

'Careful!' he shouted, to himself perhaps as much as to me, and hauled me up close in a comical, frightened embrace.

'Thank you.' I felt as if I had been too suddenly wakened from a beckoning dream, not really sure what had happened. 'I must have sat on a rotten board.'

The young man went over to where I had been sitting and leaned out, but could see nothing, he said.

'You must have been too close to the edge. Good job we were passing, eh Nancy?'

The girl stood with her hand still pressed to her throat like a singer in a melodrama. She gave me a strange look, I thought, as they passed and walked on.

I have not been back there since – I use the new bridge at the other end if I need to cross the lagoon, or walk around to the old park and sit under the willows on the crumbling banks, with their cover of leaf mould and river sludge. Yet that was a long time ago – years now – and it is silly to be still frightened of such a small accident. Though people do drown off that bridge. I have kept cuttings in a drawer, and there have been two or three deaths since the time I nearly fell in. Drunks falling through rotted railings, or leaning too far over to piss, perhaps.

The drawer is nearly full of my cuttings now. I began keeping them after my niece, Kate Lloyd, was murdered. I read it in the newspaper before their letter came from home to tell me. She was found with her throat cut and her murderer, a young man employed by the family, dead beside her, suicided. She was named after me. I kept it from Billy – Freddie was only a few months old then and I did not want to spoil anything, superstitiously. But I cut out the article and put it in the dresser, and when Maggie's letter came telling me all about it, I kept that too, tying them together with a black ribbon. My sister said she was lovely, cheeky and careless, unruly as we all had been as children. I would not think of the red blood trickling into the dust, or the soft young throat gashed open to the flies. I kneaded and pinched and cradled the flesh of my own plump infant and forced myself to think only of him.

❧

Clara came one day while I was still at the Farmers' and said we would have to decide about the old house in Rankin Street – the landlord would not keep it for us much longer, although we still paid the rent. He said he wanted someone living there so it would not fall to rack and ruin or be broken into by the larrikins who paraded drunk on horseback up and down the road on Saturday nights.

I was not drinking and now that Gertie had started to crawl about and was pretty and lovable, I thought I was ready to take up my life again. I moved quickly, while Bill was still away – I was afraid he would not agree that I was able to. Ethel and Maude and I cleaned the house from top to bottom – it seemed easy then – and we painted the children's beds with fresh paint and made new curtains from remnants I got cheap from Mr Prow.

When Bill came home he was anxious and angry at first, but gradually became easier as he saw how well things were going. He had made some money on that trip, having fallen in with some prospectors and shared their find, and he said he would stay for a while. We even talked of opening the stables again, since I said the only thing I needed now to make me happy was the horses. But in the end we did not have the money – I think we had grown too used to living apart and neither of us really wanted to change it. But for a few months we were well off and took the children on excursions, to the shows, and to the circus when it was camped on South Circle Park. Sometimes Bill and I even went to the dance hall at the Victoria, and Clara would take the kiddies into her place for the night. It was a good time, but when Bill said he should get back on the road we were happy enough to part again.

❧

One afternoon, soon after Bill had left, Clara came into my place with a funny look on her face.

'What's the matter?' I said. I was sitting on the back verandah with the cat purring on my knee in the sunshine, the children playing in the garden with the new kittens.

'There's a show coming,' she said, and hesitated a little. 'It's called *The Kelly Gang* – they're setting it up in the park. They've even got an act in it called 'The Brave Sisters and Their Part In the Outbreak'. She was more worried than I was, then. I did not think I could still be harmed by all that.

I laughed. 'Oh, I don't care any more. And no one will know that it's got anything to do with me. Unless you tell.'

Seeing that I was truthfully not upset, she persuaded me

to walk over with her to the park and watch them setting up the tents. It was a golden day in early summer, and Freddie ran along in front of us. I wheeled the baby in her pram.

The main tent, where the play would be performed, was not yet fully up, but there was a smaller tent of exhibits and posters nearby which they had finished, and they were already charging threepence to go through and look. We paid our money, but then I did hesitate. As Clara lifted the flap to let me through, holding the wriggling baby, I suddenly realised what I might be going to see.

Along one canvas wall there were photographs pinned up, and I told Clara to walk along there first and warn me if there was anything that might upset me.

'What sort of thing?' she said in a worried whisper.

'Just, anything you think I should not see.'

But it was too late. Freddie had found a picture of Edward, and said loudly to a woman standing in front of it, 'Who's that bloke?'

'That's the fierce outlaw, Ned Kelly,' she said. 'And if you aren't good his ghost will come and get you.'

'Is that my uncle?' he said to me, and I laughed with the others in the tent while I tried to shush him.

'No. No.' I put my hand over his mouth. 'Your uncle Edward is nothing like that.' But I thought people looked at me strangely.

Then I had to step up to the picture myself to show I was not concerned, and when I saw it closely I nearly fell down in a faint. Clara held my arm and took the baby from me.

'What is it Kate? What's the matter?'

I could not tell her with everyone looking on. 'Oh, only women's troubles,' I whispered back loudly enough for the woman standing next to us to hear, so that she gave me a sympathetic smile and moved away.

I did not look at the other pictures and only pretended to examine the 'Wanted' posters and the neckerchiefs they

133

claimed came from my brothers. It was not until we were nearly home that I told Clara about the photograph. I was sure, and am to this day, that it was one I left in a chemist's in Albury, one of the last taken of my brother alive, before Glenrowan, part of a set that had pictures of Joe, too, that I was too cowardly in the end to collect in case the chemist had recognised the men. It is a smallheartedness in myself I have always regretted.

The show played for some weeks, and finally Clara talked me into going with her. I cannot believe that she took money from them to bring me there, but otherwise I cannot understand how they knew I would be part of the audience.

It was a show full of lies and grand statements, and I was very amused by the painted harridan they had playing myself as a young girl. She was forever striding about the stage and clapping one hand to her forehead, groaning, 'O, my brothers, what will become of you if the evil police ever catch you up?'. We all appeared ninnies, even the men, and the songs were crude and badly sung. It should not have been a night to worry me.

But when they took their bows at the end, the leader of the troupe, a Mr Cole, came forward with his hand held up for silence.

'Ladies and gentlemen,' he shouted. 'Thank you for your appreciation indeed. But do you know ...' he paused and swept off his top hat. 'Do you know? Are you aware? That the notorious Kate Kelly herself, sister of the infamous Ned, sits actually amongst you this very night? Yes, actually amongst you respectable citizens of Forbes ...'

I shrank down in my seat but he was pointing at me, and people were craning round to see who it was. Clara stood up with me, I will say that for her, and we left hurriedly, stumbling over the feet of people who tried to stop us going.

'No. No. He's wrong.' I kept saying loudly, my hand up over my face, as we made our way out of the tent. 'He is wrong. I am not Kate Kelly. No, no.' And I went on saying it out in the street and on the way home so that people stopped and stared at me and Clara became very worried.

When we got back to her place I collapsed on an armchair. The children were with their grandmother.

'Please Clara,' I said. 'I must have a drink. Just one. Please. You see how upset I have been.'

She was upset herself – and feeling guilty I have always thought – and after one doubtful look she went for the bottle.

We drank until I passed out, sobbing, with Clara's arms around me, rocking me gently, trying to soothe away the humiliation. And in the corner of my eye as I slipped into blessed forgetfulness, flickered the picture I have always sought to avoid looking at direct since I saw it first, the picture of Joe that I sensed hung on the wall of the tent beside my brothers, that travesty of Joe, dead, leant against the station wall at Glenrowan while they took their filthy pictures, and I knew the time of peace was over for me once more ...

Kate became cunning this time. She was not going to let them put her back in the hospital with its ice-baths and twisted ropes of wet bedsheets and the sickening gruel they forced down her throat at all hours. So she managed to hold off her drinking now until the evening. And she forced herself, every day, to go through the motions of keeping the house clean and the children fed and clothed. In the morning when she first woke up, blurred and scratchy from the night before, she lay in bed going over and over the things she would have to do that day until they were imprinted firmly on her memory – make the breakfast, bread and dripping; dress the children, clean underclothes; take Freddie to school; buy meat and bread at the corner shop on the way home with the little girl; wash the dishes; tidy the beds and pick up the dropped heaps of clothing from yesterday; feed the cat; darn Gertie's stockings; make lunch for them both; walk in the park and sit on the warm grass and watch Gertie play – a time when the mind can go thankfully blank; don't let the little girl stray too close to the water's edge, she might fall in and drown (her gaping mouth . . .); collect Freddie from school; make supper; put the children to bed.

Then . . . the gin bottle hovered in her mind, clear and shining. Then, she promised herself in those dreary aching mornings, striving for clarity, then, when I have done everything else properly. Then . . .

She thought it was the Pink Pills that caused her back pains, so she changed her brand and bought Holloways tablets, advertised for debilitated constitutions. The backaches did not really go away, but the new tablets seemed to help in other ways, to give her energy for an hour or two after taking them, enough to get through the housework, and they seemed to make the day go faster.

She began to collect the newspaper clippings again. In the evenings, with the children in bed and the gin bottle gleaming in the lantern light on the table near her hand, she went through the *Gazette*.

Nearly every night there was something that interested her, that she would cut out carefully with her sharp silver scissors and fold into a neat oblong with the others in the drawer. Sometimes it was only an advertisement for a show or a diorama that took her fancy – *The Tour of the Prince of Wales in India*, or slides of the Russo-Turco War, with sounds of real gunfire, or *The Reproduction of Jerusalem and The Crucifixion, by Limelight*. Perhaps she intended to take the children some night but she never did. And gradually her interests narrowed and became sour.

She cut out and read two or three times the article about

the body of a man found near Bobadah, five months dead at least, who had probably succumbed to thirst. She was drawn at first to stories of drought, of parching. Another man had died on the plains near Pangee Run, also, it was assumed, of thirst, although his body had been too badly mutilated by wild dogs to be certain. Somehow the image of his bleached, incomplete skeleton turning slowly in its own dust in the desert, comforted her. Then she began to read stories of drownings, avidly, as if the rest had only been a preliminary.

A travelling salesman had drowned off the Forbes River bridge near the old lagoon. He was drunk, those who saw him leave the hotel earlier in the evening testified. The body of a tramp was washed halfway up the banks of the river downstream, where she and Bill had sometimes gone for picnics, the corpse already decomposed. They thought the rising of the river had lifted a log or the detritus that had imprisoned and hidden his body, finally allowing the disgusting remains to float free.

She walked to the sites of some of these drownings – a surprising number of them were nearby – and she saw how the lagoon had swelled with the sudden rain. Leaning on the rails of the old bridge, where she had not been for years, trying to imagine the force which would propel a drunken body outwards and over into the dirty cold water, she saw how the dusty banks, eroded by the long drought, sent oozing runnels of mud into the river. The mosquitoes hummed and gathered in the puddles around the lagoon's edge; dead birds and young, half-eaten animals ringed the water's rim. There was a greasy meniscus on the tide. Six men had died in a shearing-shed, of influenza. The drains through the township ran muddy and acrid; at dusk you could see the slithering rats. There was a typhoid scare . . .

At night sometimes, she slipped out, the gin bottle firmly under her arm, and sat on the banks under the willows watching the fluorescent ebb and flow of the tide, sipping her comforting drink, and deliberately, now, drifting back into dreams of those days by that other river, towards the end, when Steve and Dan were hardly ever sober, nor she herself. Only Ned stayed apart, sternly, his white face and glittering, haunted eyes accusing them for their weakness. Joe drank with her, but he never got drunk. She thought, even then, he knew what was coming, and drank with her to comfort her, although he tried to argue with her, too.

'Don't take to the drink, Kitty. It'll do you no good, ever.'

But she was young and wild, and there was desperation in everything they did, then.

'I have to, don't you see, Joe?' She spoke aloud, whined, in the dark night beside the swelling lagoon.

'I am afraid, Joe. What is to become of us all? It is not a game any more, is it? I'm afraid, you see. The drink helps.' She took another mouthful from the bottle.

'Don't be angry. Joe?' She wheedled, and twisted round where she sat, clasping the trunk of the old willow, pressing her lips to its roughened bark, swooning into an open-mouthed kiss, her hand between her legs rubbing and pushing, imitating and finally achieving some sort of lover's release, a furtive, shuddering climax that often left her crying weakly, struggling to hold the picture of the tall young man rushing towards her with the garland of eucalyptus leaves in his dull gold hair.

Once, after one of these nights, she woke in the stiff, cold dawn. A man, Chinese, dressed in coarse grey trousers and jacket, his fishing pole over his shoulders, squatted nearby watching her. He did not move while she gathered her things together and shook her cramped arms, dropping the empty bottle from the crook of her elbow as she backed away, holding her shawl tightly about her shivering body, and turning, hurrying off into the grey greening light.

4

Bill has taken to staying away for three or four months at a time, sending us money, and only here a week or two when he does come home. I take good care to conceal my drinking when he is here, but I saw by the way he watched me last time that he was not convinced. Perhaps he has a woman somewhere else. I don't blame him for that, although he was kind to me this visit - too kind perhaps, as now I am expecting this child.

Another man drowned in January, near the lake. There were floods after all the rain we had in summer, and the reservoir overflowed. The streets ran with the dirty water for weeks and people wrote into the *Gazette* to complain. I have cut out some of their letters. There are rats around all the streets at night, feeding off the refuse in the gutters.

I was sick for a while, and I was afraid at first it was the typhoid, not knowing I was expecting. The children must be watched very carefully now. There have been cases in the hospital of children with the disease and there has been an epidemic in Sydney. The mosquitoes are bad for this time of year, too, the middle of autumn is it? Although the heat and stillness are left over from the summer. Clara says she was talking to the butcher and his brother told him there is a cool change coming from up the river. I hope it does not bring more rain, or there will be the floods again, and more drownings no doubt.

I have not been out for some days, since the article I saw about the bushranger in the paper. A man named Kelly, too, has been released from jail somewhere, and Clara asked me if it was another brother of mine. She is not my friend any more. I think she asked it purely out of malice, knowing I have only the one brother left – Jim – and when will I ever see them all again?

Maude and Ethel seem also to have drawn away from me and look at me strangely. I do not think they can have found out I am back to the drink, I have been very careful. But sometimes I feel I have lost the thread of what I am saying, and it is then that they stare at me. 'Tunnels? What tunnels?' Ethel said yesterday and I realised I had let my night-time world bleed into this other grey, unreal life I drag myself through day by day. I have found a little cave, in the roots of an old tree, that is just like the tunnels we dug all around our camp and hid in sometimes, close and dark and safe.

It is being pregnant, that's all. I remember feeling vague and blurred with Gertie, too. My body is too heavy to drag about already, and my mind will not stay on what I am doing. God I am dreading the winter, getting the wood from the pile, cleaning the grate, the chill and the sharp ache always in my back, getting worse and worse as the child grows weightier – not even the pills helping any more . . .

Sometimes I think it is Joe's child I am growing here. When Bill was home and we lay in bed at night I thought of Joe. I dreamt it was Joe's young, silvered body that I held, and that we lay on a bed of twigs and leaves and his hair shone in the moonlight. Otherwise I could not bear Bill's lifeless hands to touch me, and my flesh would fall away from his caress. This way it gave him pleasure, too, and he left saying he would not be away so long this time – he was pleased that I seemed happier than before, he said.

Before, I used to lie in bed, rigid, letting his rough hands explore my body, cringing from his weight on top of me. I tried to remain quite silent through it, not letting even my breathing sound in case he thought I was encouraging, or even welcoming his attentions. But this last time it was easy; I am surprised it has taken me all these years to find the way to pleasure. But I have felt closer to Joe this year, as if his spirit has returned and is hovering near me. I tried to explain it to Clara one day, without telling her of Joe, but only that I thought perhaps people could return from the dead when you needed them, and stay with you for a while. She laughed at me and said she hoped I had not been paying good money to see the old madwoman down by the railway line who advertises that she can put you in touch with the spirit life.

No one understands. When I lay with Bill I knew it was only his outer husk in my bed, that somehow Joe had found a way to inhabit Bill's body and that it was really him I lay with, caressing and kissing, our limbs wound round like tender vines. If Bill found me changed it is only because of this change in him that he does not know about. Now, sometimes, I feel that I am waiting, that one day if I concentrate and do not lose faith, I will see him truly, Joe, in his leather breeches and cowboy's leggings striding through the misty trees in the morning . . .

And I believe he comes to me at night now, when I am alone, although I wake in a cold bed. But I wake remembering the pleasure of the darkness, and my skin still glows from the warmth of his young body. His hands hold my breast gently and smooth the mound of my belly, and his fingers pry into the secret places beneath. Those are things I could not imagine. 'Kitty, love,' he whispers to me in the night. 'Kitty my love.' And I wake with his voice in my ear. He has been through the fire, my Joe, and found his way back to me ...

⌒

Kate rose heavily from where she had been sitting at the kitchen table, cutting items from the newspaper. She leant for a moment on the table top, then gathered up the scraps she had cut out and squared them neatly, tying them with a brown grosgrain ribbon before putting them in the dresser drawer, carefully aligned beneath dockets and other similiar packets.

The kitchen was dim and untidy. With Bill away so much she made less and less effort in the house, rarely cooking, feeding herself and the children on bread and cheese or dripping, and sometimes a pennyworth of hot food from the grocer's on the corner.

When the children were in bed, like now, she would settle in her dingy, undusted front room, with only one lamp lit so that she did not have to notice the drifts of dust and fluff in the corners or the draped cobwebs on the top of the mantel-piece and cupboards.

She sat in the rocking-chair Bill's mother had given them when they married, her swollen belly creating a grotesque humped shadow in the flickering lamplight. On her lap was a scrap of knitting that she had started months ago when she first learned of this new child coming and which had not pro-gressed beyond the first few cobbled inches. She sat gently rocking, her eyes half closed, her body still except for the occasional reaching out for the gin bottle when the glass she regularly raised to her lips was empty.

Finally she put the glass down with a sigh – the bottle was nearly half full but she was again trying to keep the drinking down. Bill was expected back in the next few days. She took the bottle and the glass back to the kitchen where she rinsed

142

one and hid the other behind the tea caddy in the dresser. She checked that her secret supply was still there in a bottle marked 'vinegar', letting her fingers stroke its smooth stony sides before she shut the cupboard door.

She went slowly, ponderously, along the passage to the children's room. They were both asleep, their pale faces gleaming in the moonlight filtered through the badly drawn curtains. She leant on the doorframe watching for a moment, staring at their faces as they slept. She kept meaning to take them to the park to see the animals, but somehow she never seemed to have the time. Perhaps tomorrow. She must try to remember.

She washed, the cold flannel sobering her enough to make her walk back to the kitchen to make sure she had put out all the lamps. In darkness she went back to her own bedroom and undressed down to her stretched and grimy shift. She fell into a deep, dreamless sleep as soon as she closed her eyes.

Maude and Ethel were worried about her and finally they wrote to Bill:

We don't know what to do about her, she is not ill but she is not really what you might call well either. We don't think she is on the grog but she seems so far away from everything, and talks as if she is a young girl again living in the bush with her brothers. Perhaps you better come back soon if you can and see what you think. The kiddies are well, no need to worry on their account . . .

☙

In late April he came back and stayed a fortnight. But Kate was very careful with him there, and he could see nothing wrong that he could put his finger on except that she was vaguer than usual. He was easily persuaded that that was the effect of the pregnancy. He had a big job to go to at Burrawang and was anxious to start. He allowed himself to believe

143

that it would all turn out all right. His life away from Kate and the children had gradually assumed more importance to him anyway – a world of horses and work and pubs which they formed no part of, even in his thoughts.

One day while he was home they went to see Probasco's Circus, finally, which was camped in a vacant block behind the hotel, with its 'talking' horse and clowns and a Wild West Act.

The children were fascinated by the cowboys and cowgirls in buckskins on their leaping horses. One woman rode two abreast, standing up on the horses' backs, one foot on each, twirling a lariat and hallooing loudly. Kate muttered during this and the children had to tell her to hush.

'I could outride these buggers when I was a girl,' she said to the little boy, and he looked disbelievingly at her bulging stomach and the pale, lifeless hands on his shoulder. She laughed at his expression but she wished she had taken more time to teach the children to ride, to show them what she was talking about. After the baby is born perhaps, she thought, but with no real conviction. She knew she had little time now.

Otherwise she seemed to enjoy the day as much as the little ones, laughing when the talking horse swore at its trainer, greeting friends, her face easy and relaxed as they strolled home in the dusk, licking delicately at their coloured ices.

But in the night she woke, crying out, 'Joe! Joe! Listen to the horses . . .'. Bill held her until she calmed down and slid back into sleep. He was not a man given to much questioning – it was a nightmare, no need to explain that, he was satisfied. In the morning he told her about it, but she looked at him blankly and said she could not remember.

☙

In May the drought still had not broken; dust-storms swirled in the over-cultivated paddocks and blew through the streets of the town. Depending on the direction of the wind you could smell the lagoon for miles. Filth and sewage floated on the turgid water, breasted majestically by three swans that came from nowhere and settled on the lake.

The weather was cold, but not like real winter, everyone agreed. More like a chilly summer, and the sun was hot enough at noon. A diphtheria outbreak carried off the blacksmith, and the schools closed for a week until they were sure it was not an epidemic.

Bill rode off to his new job on the morning after some rain had come at last, but the sun was out already, baking the muddy pools that lay along the road. Kate stood by the parlour window, the lace curtain drooping in her fingers, watching his wagon turn the corner out of Rankin Street. He had promised to be back in time for the baby's birth. She did not care. His visit had disrupted the rhythms of her growing fantasies, although his body in her bed at night gave them flesh.

As soon as she saw he was truly gone she went to the kitchen dresser and took down the bottle marked 'vinegar'. She pulled the cork and drank deeply. She had not had any gin for the whole fortnight Bill had been home, making do with frequent sipping from her bottle of sweet pink medicine instead. She shuddered as the sharp subtle alcohol slid down her throat, stood still for a moment to feel its cold turn to warmth spreading through her organs, and put the bottle back. Tonight, she promised herself. Tonight, Joe . . .

◠

We have been waiting so long for the rain, and now that it is here it is too much like drowning. All I can see from the window is the water washing down and down out of the brown sky. They kept my brother Edward in rotting hulks at Williamstown when they said they were taking him to Pentridge, and for six months he lay on planks just below the water line and looked out at the murky flotsam of the harbour catching on the trapped seaweed around the boat, so that the same piece of decaying wood might bob there for days, he said, tapping against the porthole, although he was lucky to have one to look out of at all, most did not ... It is the weight of the water, it presses down. The house seems drained of air; if I opened a window or a door my breath would be sucked from me into the flood.

It seems that I have stayed by this cascading window since Bill left, days, or is it weeks ago. The time goes by and I do not notice it. The children avoid me – they go next door to Clara's or down the hill to their grandmother and aunts. Or they creep about the house as they are doing now and play secret games in rooms they know I will not enter. Fred opened this door yesterday by mistake and thought he withdrew quickly enough for me not to notice, but I do. It doesn't matter, it is a time we must all get through somehow, and then it will be all right.

I did not go to bed at all last night, but sat in the armchair here by the window, watching. Sometimes the downpour eased, or stopped almost altogether and I thought of going out and walking by the lagoon to see if the rain has cleared away the filth as it sometimes does. It is a long time since the water was high enough to lap the banks all silver in the moonlight. But I did not go. I was too tired and afraid I might slip on the wet rocks of the path – not for my sake, but for this baby that kicks and turns sluggishly inside my body.

My breasts have grown again, large and full, and Joe laughs sometimes at how different they are from before, but he likes them and pretends to suck, saying that it will stimulate the milk for the child; but the way he kneads and crushes is not childlike. Of course it is not Joe, squeezing my heavy breasts in his cupped, tender hands, bending to kiss my neck, rubbing the huge swell of my belly, deftly parting the hidden lips of that other eager place, I know it is not him. But it could be. It could have been. Oh God, Joe, we have blighted our lives,

146

all of us. We will not escape this time. They will hunt us down and corner us and put fire to us and set us screaming in pain and fear; and the women and girls will be left as always, with the dryness ever at the back of their throats and the dark spaces in our heads where the flames crackle and echo and golden fire whooshes through the cracks of the mind. Joe, why did you leave me? Why did you let them take you and defile you? Why will you not leave me now? Must I drag myself after you burning in my brain for the rest of my life?

~

After the baby was born, Clara saw with relief that Kate seemed better. She said so to Bill, who had come back in time for the birth but could only stay a week or so. Kate did not seem to reject this child – as she had Gertie at first – but lay placidly, staring into the pearly unfocused eyes, her own gaze sharp and tender as it had not been for some time.

But in the third week the child became ill and would not suck. Clara sent for the doctor, and Kate watched with a sort of knowing apathy as he examined the baby, his hand moving too often to the fevered forehead. Although she had not been feeding well, the infant's belly was bloated, her faeces watery and foul-smelling.

'What is it then?' Kate said at last, although she guessed. The rains had finally stopped, and spring had brought heat and flies and blocked up water mains. The gutters again lay under a luminous film of mud and excrement.

'It's typhoid,' he said, and hastily added, 'but not too serious. We will try the new treatment on her – it has worked well with others. She must be weaned and fed only boiled water for a day or two. Then boiled milk from a bottle.' The doctor saw Kate's expression, and added, 'She will be all right, I promise. We have caught it in time, I think.'

Perhaps it was the weaning, Clara thought, that brought

147

back Kate's despair. Even when the baby began to recover she never seemed to regain her pleasure in the child. She complained to Clara about her.

'She won't suck the bottle properly.' Her own milk had dried, painfully. 'She turns her head away, and I have to force the teat down her throat.'

She seemed to think the baby acted deliberately, out of spite. Why else would she wake three or four times in the night, bleating with hunger, and then refuse more than an ounce or two of the tediously boiled and cooled goats' milk? She was not thriving, and Kate had hoped to have a fat, lusty infant to show Joe when he came back. Joe? No, she meant Bill, of course. She sat in tears by the grey window, watching the dawn redden the rooftops of the houses opposite, helpless to stop the baby's fretful crying, deserted, she felt, by everyone. Even Joe. Where was he? Why did he not come?

Clara was impatient with her and horrified at the things she said.

'Don't ever say you don't like your own baby, Kate. That will bring you nothing but bad luck. Poor little thing.' She lifted the blankets from around the baby's face. 'She'll be all right. Won't you, little one?' she turned, showing Kate the small sleeping face, but she was not watching. She stood staring out of the window, towards the park and the lagoon, as if she truly had no interest at all in the small bundle. 'Kate, you will feel better soon. Don't take it out on this poor wee scrap.'

Kate still would not turn – her listlessness these days was almost total.

'It's true, I don't like her,' she said in a flattened voice. 'She will not drink her milk when I go to all the trouble of making it for her. She cries all night and won't let me rest.'

But she took the baby when Clara handed it to her and sat by the window, holding the bottle to its mouth with a sort of martyred indifference. Clara was glad to slip away home.

5

BILL CAME BACK unexpectedly last week and of course found me drinking. Oh the quarrelling, the endless words, they drive me mad, they get in the way of everything ... It is the end, this time, he said. He will finish this job and come back and he will take the children off me. I am not fit to be their mother. What does he mean, this fool of a man, with words like 'mother'? What does he understand? Nothing at all. But I wept and wept – he expected it – and promised once more. Oh I would promise anything to be free of the words, the people, they drag me down, when I want only to drift away ... to Joe ... he is real ... I emptied all the bottles in front of Bill, at least he thought it was all. I said I only drank because I am worried about the baby, but I am not now, any more. She will be all right, everything will be all right, Joe has promised. But something must happen soon – Bill threatens to come home every Saturday now, to make sure I do not break my promises. Joe must come for me soon, I could not bear those two days away from him every week, and if I do not drink I will not be able to summon him ...

Perhaps it was Clara's impatience with her that led Kate to turn to her other neighbour, Susan Healey, when she at last decided to act. She had left the children with Susan before, but never the baby, and Susan was a little taken aback to be asked to mind them all overnight.

'It is all right.' Kate swayed a little in the doorway of the little house which smelled nicely of floor polish and baking. Her speech was slurred with the gin and the pills she had already taken that morning. The children stood pale and silent, holding her skirt. The baby was hastily bundled in an old blanket. Kate held it out to Susan Healey, who reached for it automatically.

'Their father will be back tomorrow, or the next day. I forget . . . But if I'm not back by then he will give you more money.' She had already pressed into the reluctant woman's hand the six shillings Bill had left this last time.

'Please . . . Susan.' She lurched and held onto the door frame for support. 'I must get away. Only for a day or two. I must think . . . please. I must have time to get myself straight.' Her voice became cunning, wheedling. 'The baby is recovered now, she will be no trouble. But don't let Bill's mother know, that's all. Please . . .'

Susan was to say later that she was half frightened by Kate's dishevelled earnestness, the feeling that she would do something . . . awful, if she, Susan, did not agree to do what was asked. And Kate's relief and gratitude, when Susan finally did agree, partly mollified her, at the time.

Kate bent to kiss the children.

'Goodbye. I will leave a note for your father in case I'm not back. He is on his way,' she said again to Susan. 'I sent him a message to come . . .'

Susan shut her door after she saw Kate's uncertain figure reach her own house safely. Shaking her head, she went into her kitchen and began to prepare a bottle for the crying baby.

150

The evening hung heavily over the lake, grey clouds rising and swelling across the sky, the trees barely swaying in the light breeze, their silhouettes darkening gradually with the dusk. The old Chinese man, with his fishing basket, peered into the shadows beneath the old trees behind the lagoon as he came across the bridge. He could not see whatever it was he thought moved there, just a flash of lighter grey in the gathering darkness. It was not the right time for the woman he sometimes saw in that exact spot; that was always in the middle of the night, before dawn, when he came to set up his lines.

∾

Kate shifted herself back into the cave of the huge gnarled roots. She had spread out her shawl to sit on and she hummed quietly to herself as she wriggled and settled like an animal in its lair. She had two full, new bottles of gin and the whole night to wait for Joe. She was sure he would come tonight – it was the crying of the baby that had kept him away, afraid it might bring the coppers after him . . .

Tonight he will come, and if he asks again, tonight she will go with him. She has made up her mind. Instead of huddling in a crying heap when he leaves, drawing his smooth body from her clinging arms before the sun can rise on their love, she will follow his fading, beckoning form as he retreats, melting into the morning fog that rises from the river banks.

She unscrews the stopper from the first bottle and raises it to her lips, her eyes half shut in the pleasure of that first numbing mouthful. She has not had a drink for hours, since she took the children next door to Susan's. The night falls suddenly, there is no light inside her little cave. She loosens her hair and unfastens the neck of her blouse. She lies, langorously, waiting . . .

∾

Another morning grew still and grey out of the warm sunrise.

151

The old Chinese man made his way again across the old bridge, not noticing the decomposing carcasses of dogs and cats and other small things lying half submerged on the edge of the slyly lapping lagoon, the weeping willows in full green leaf leaning towards their watery reflections. It was going to be another hot day, despite the clouds; the oily water slid softly under the bridge, slapping and falling around the wooden uprights.

Beside the old rotting log downsteam, its jagged edge poking out of the water into the mud, the greasy tide tugged futilely at a new piece of flotsam jammed hard against the bank, the free end rocking listlessly with the waves. It was the woman, floating face down, but he could recognise her. Her fine black hair had washed backwards under the clothing that had also somehow become draped around her neck and over her head, caught against the log, leaving her pale back bare. Her skirt lifted and eddied like washing in a tub where it did not cling to her strong legs and buttocks. Her exposed calves and feet gleamed white, ludicrously buoyant. In the middle of the bridge, on the broken railing, was an empty gin bottle, already in the hot morning attracting a cloud of flies and midges to its rim.

The old man backed slowly away, his hand to his mouth, tripping over rubbish at the edge of the water, then turning, ran, with his old man's stooping run, back to the waving tall gums and the clearing blue sky of the town.